I lost my mobile at the mall

Teenager on the edge of technological breakdown

I lost my mobile at the mall

Teenager on the edge of technological breakdown

wendy harmer

Kane Miller
A DIVISION OF EDC PUBLISHING

CSCL

First American Edition 2011
Kane Miller, A Division of EDC Publishing

First published by Random House Australia in 2009
Copyright © Out of Harms Way Pty Ltd 2009
Cover photograph courtesy Photolibrary
Cover design by Ellie Exarchos

For information contact:
Kane Miller, A Division of EDC Publishing
PO Box 470663
Tulsa, OK 74147-0663
www.kanemiller.com
www.edcpub.com

Quotes on pp 200, 201 from *Jane Eyre* (1847) by Charlotte Brontë (1816–1855)
Quotes on pp 77, 112, 113, 156 from *The Art of War* by Sun Tzu, translated by
Lionel Giles. Copyright unknown.

Library of Congress Control Number: 2010933234

Printed and bound in the United States of America
1 2 3 4 5 6 7 8 9 10
ISBN: 978-1-935279-97-6

For Maeve and Marley
☺ ILY4EXXXX

Saturday afternoon.

My name is Elly Pickering. I've lost my mobile phone at the mall and am now facing certain death.

There are many ways a healthy fifteen-year-old girl can die. I'll list a few of them here.

I have lost my mobile phone so …

1. My mother will kill me.
OK, she won't try to actually, physically, murder me – she's shorter than me, can't run as fast as me, and won't be able to find an axe until she finds her reading glasses. But in some ways, a sharp, fatal blow to the head would be better than the excruciating long-term abuse that will follow when I break the news. She will accuse me of being lazy, ungrateful, negligent and plain old stupid.

The idea that reading glasses can disappear in exactly the same circumstances will not occur to my mother. The first death I suffer will be from an utter lack of natural justice.

2. My father will kill me.

My father's part in my death will be more subtle, but just as effective. He will sentence me to die by disappointment. He will not be angry. He won't want to find a blunt instrument and cave in my skull. Instead he'll be "let down." His eyes will look to his lap, his shoulders will sag and there will be a long, loud escape of air from his chest, as if I have crept up behind him and pulled out his plug. He will crumple like a punctured bouncy castle. This is the third time I've lost my mobile and I'm sure my father thinks I deliberately throw it down a well to prove to him that there is no God.

3. My best friend will kill me.

Bianca will try to actually, physically, murder me. She stabbed me with a pen once when I borrowed her suede skirt and ripped a hole in it. The pen punctured the skin on my thigh and drew blood, the ink went into the muscle tissue and now I have the world's tiniest tattoo. I will have this mark for life … and all for a misdemeanor on the hide of a cow that was already dead!

She will probably try to suffocate me with a pillow

(no incriminating strangle marks) if I ever fall asleep anywhere near her – and all because there is a photo in my mobile of her standing next to Hugh Jackman. (OK, losing this is a capital offense, but she is supposed to be my BF and should show mercy.)

There is also a text in there from Jai that he sent to me by mistake on the first night he and Bianca got together. I've been promising for six months to send her the photo and text, but I've been busy. So kill me!

Bianca will kill me, that's for sure, and no one will have any evidence to convict her of the crime. The "Exhibit A" of my phone could be in the lost and found box at the mall and lie there undiscovered for years until the whole thing is exposed on one of those *Cold Case File* shows on TV. But by then it will be too late.

I will be long dead.

4. My boyfriend will kill me.

This will be death from the grief of a broken heart. BTW, I didn't mention that I also lost my entire handbag and that the friendship ring Will bought me was in it. It's silver, carved with leaves and has tiny blue stones on it. Like something Arwen Evenstar might wear on an Elves' Night Out in Lothlórien. (*Lord of the Rings* is my fave movie and book.)

The ring's very, very gorgeous.

The only reason I wasn't wearing it is because I was

at the cosmetics counter trying some hand cream that is supposed to whiten your skin so you can actually have hands that look like Arwen's (or Liv's) and I didn't want to get gunk on it.

Now it's gone. I don't even want to think what Will might say. It's my first piece of jewelry from a boy, ever. And it's the first piece of jewelry he has given a girl, ever. So who will die from a broken heart first – me or him – no one can tell. This could be a double homicide. (Technically not quite right, but you know what I mean.)

5. I will kill myself.
I am not a particularly dramatic person, but all my numbers, texts and photos were in my phone (one year's worth), and if I don't get them back my life is not worth living.

Saturday. 3 p.m.
Three hours PM (post mobile).

I haven't had my phone for three hours now.

Of course the first thing I did when I got home from the mall was to go on FacePlace and send out an emergency bulletin informing my 105 friends (including the Prime Minister of Australia) that as of midday I am uncontactable by phone. (Our house doesn't have a landline – my mum, dad and my older sister, Tilly, all have mobiles.)

I also said in the bulletin that if anyone gets a ring from my phone it's not me. Further to that, I advised that if they do get a call from my phone, they should keep the criminal on the line as long as possible, then ring 000 from another line so the police can track down their exact whereabouts, surround them and send in a SWAT team.

Then I put up a new picture of myself on FacePlace. I like this pic. It's just a close-up of me smiling. I have suntanned skin, you can see a sparkle in my green eyes and my eyelashes are looking almost like a mascara ad. My long brown hair is curling over my shoulders in waves and looks really shiny. I am wearing a black tank top and my arms look slim. All in all, this is a good pic. Will took it on my camera, so that makes it extra special.

Then I Googled "lost mobile" and got 17,000,000 results. I found the five steps to follow when someone's ripped off your phone – given that it's entirely unlikely that I have lost it.

1. Phone the number immediately.
Couldn't do that 'cos I have no phone. *Der!*

2. Report the phone missing.
See above. *Der!*

3. Call 1800 LOST and get a block on the phone.
Der! No phone!!

4. Replace the phone.
This is not going to be as easy as it sounds. I looked in my jewelry box and I have $13.50. I found a birthday card from Nan with a $20 bill inside. There was $8.50 in change on my bedside table which brings my total worth

to $42. So Mum and Dad will just buy me a new one.
Right? *Der!*

Then I looked at some glitter eye shadow you can order
online. It comes from New York in 3–4 working days.

Then I got bored.

Remember what it was like when you lost a baby tooth
and your tongue just couldn't help itself from exploring
the new squishy gap in your gum? My fingers are like that.
They're out to explore without any supervision from me and
keep reaching for the phone that isn't there. Tap-tap-tapping
on the non-existent keypad.

:(HLP me. Im dyng.

People who have had their arms and legs amputated say
that sometimes it feels like the missing bit is still attached.
As if the nerves from their limbs are still firing electronic
impulses to their brains. Then they try to scratch an itch and
just swipe at empty air.

My phone's been amputated. I can feel it vibrating in
my pocket, *beep-beeping* with a message or ringing in my
ears, and I turn and reach for it, but it's gone.

Gone for three whole hours. That's one hundred and
eighty minutes or 10,800 seconds. Your life could totally
change in that time. That's if you had any way of knowing.

One hundred and eighty minutes is also how long it took
to watch the movie *Australia* (which seemed like for-ev-er, but
when Bianca and I came out of the movieplex, the sun was,

amazingly, still out) and while I was in there with my phone switched off, checking out Nicole Kidman's hair, my life could have changed forever and I wouldn't have known.

That is entirely possible. Think about it.

In that time I could have had a call from Will saying that he loved me.

ILY4E

I told Will I loved him first. OK, everyone in the entire history of the earth knows that this is a BAD move. I didn't mean to say it, but it just came out.

It was yesterday after school when I was watching Will surf down at Hammerhead. I was sitting on the sand minding our stuff. Not because I am a totally downtrodden female, but because I had just combed a mango and passion fruit treatment through my hair. I was enjoying the "luxurious tropical fragrance," lying back and imagining I was in Tahiti. I didn't want to go swimming and ruin the treatment with a massive salt blast. Salt is bad for you. That's what they say. Bad for your hair. Bad for your heart. And, as I discovered, bad for your love life.

Because the thing is, it was just an ordinary summer afternoon at Hammerhead. The sky was an ordinary blue. The sand an ordinary beige. And as I watched Will trudging up the dune to where I was sitting, I just felt like my ordinary self.

And then Will leaned over me and when he did that, I saw close up that his golden curls were clumped together with tiny globs of salt. I saw that his eyes were the same soft gray as the rocks in the cliff. And then I noticed that the sun was shining through every drop of water on his skin and he seemed to be strung with fairy lights – a magical water sprite washed up on the incoming tide. And then I told him I loved him.

"Uh, towel," says Will.

And then I ran and jumped in the sea, creating a giant mango and passion fruit conditioner slick that is probably still giving wading birds in New Zealand glossier and more manageable feathers.

Ever since then, I've been waiting to be given the kiss of life. And now my mobile, my lifeline, is gone and for the past three hours I've been drifting in an open sea.

PLZHLPme. Im gng under.

I'm sitting on my bed and I can hear Mum's car coming up the driveway. It should be like the Hammerhead Surf Rescue Boat is coming to save me, but all I can think of is that when she knows I've lost my mobile, my mother will just turn around and row back to shore.

Before I tell her, I suppose I should retrace my steps to where I lost my bag. That's what Dad will say when I tell him. *Think logically, Flly. When did you have your handbag last?*

Unfortunately, the answer to this question is not in any way logical. And it's not as if I haven't been thinking about it.

Bianca and I were at the mall (Your Honor), and I know I had my bag when we were in our fave fashion store, Tiara, because I bought a braided belt with an adorable beaded buckle, paid for it, and put the belt and my wallet inside it. I remember admiring my butter-yellow squashy leather bag and thinking it reminded me of a cute Shar-Pei puppy. I gave it an affectionate pat. It really was the most good and cute and perfect bag.

The next thing I can remember (Officer) is sitting with Bianca on our usual bench. This is where we always sit to scope out the toxic tide of fashion disasters that slops up and down the mall escalators. I remember that I beat Bianca with a top score of seven positively identified fashion crimes:

1. White lace bra under black mesh tank top
    − Eeeyew! Do you even own a mirror?

2. Leopard-print scrunchie − circa 1992.

3. Gypsy skirt − banned by the United Nations last time I checked.

4. Popped collar − Wassup? You have a rash on your neck, bro?

5. Fake tan lines on legs − Road to ruin.

6. Jeans with designer rips – Shanghai Seamstress Goes Postal With Box Cutter!

7. T-shirt with "Gold Coast" spelled out in sequins – Aaargh!

Seven is a good score. Not a perfect score of ten on the hideousness index, but still, a good effort. Bianca usually beats me. She can spot a fashion crime from miles away. It's almost as if she has a built-in dreck-o-meter.

"Don't look," gasps Bianca. "White frilly socks and black patent ballet flats coming out of Cathedral Candles right this minute. I said, DON'T LOOK!"

At this point I swivel my head back around to see Bianca's bright blue eyeballs tunneling right through the soft tissue of my brain and out the back of my head. The perpetrator is then expertly tracked without any idea she has been spotted. Bianca's eyes are constantly sweeping the perimeters of the mall like floodlights on razor wire at a high security correctional facility. Even through massive sunglasses, no one, nothing, escapes her piercing gaze.

For instance – one day Bianca suspected I was wearing Disney Princess undies and barricaded me in my room until I agreed to change out of them.

"Are you in Year Nine or just nine years old?!" she fumes through the door.

After the offending Sleeping Beauty cotton glitter

knickers had been hurled in the trash and I'd pulled on black stretch boy-legs, I was allowed to proceed. You have to respect a girl who cares that much. And you *definitely* don't want her as an enemy.

Anyway, back to the mall. I'll admit that I took advantage of the fact that Bianca was texting Jai nonstop. (Ever since she met him I have only had her full attention for random three-minute intervals.) So I was the one on sentry duty. I came, I saw, I cringed and took honors with, as I say, seven fully documented style transgressions. That's how I know I still had my mobile phone. The ghastly photographs of each one are stored there.

After viewing the evidence Bianca had to admit she had been outclassed. And let me tell you, for Bianca, that was a biggie. She offered to buy me a juice from Hip Pip to celebrate and maybe … maybe that's where I lost my bag? During the resulting shock, because, believe me, Bianca NEVER admits ANYTHING.

Then we went back to Tiara one more time so Bianca could buy a silver glitter headband. After that, we left.

We boarded the bus outside the mall and when it accelerated into the middle lane before we had even sat down, I fell on top of Bianca.

"Ow! Watch it, Belly!" Bianca screeches.

Now, I have spoken to Bianca about this "Belly" business. And, you can add to that, "Nelly," "Jelly" and "Smelly." Also combinations of any of the above: "JellyBelly," "SmellyNelly" and "JellySmellyBellyNellyElly."

My full name is Eleanor. I will settle for Elly. My sister's name is Matilda. She gets "Matty," "Tilda," "Tills" and will also accept "Tilly." And that's what our family calls her – Tilly.

Eleanor and Matilda are the names of Queens of England. Why did Mum and Dad choose these names? It's a long, pathetic joke.

We live in the suburb of Oldcastle in the City of Britannia, New South Wales, Australia. Mum's name is Elizabeth (commonly known as "Libby") and Dad's name is Richard (AKA "Rick"). So somewhere along the way Mum and Dad thought it would be hilarious to imagine that our house at 25 Buckingham Street, Oldcastle, Britannia was some kind of royal palace.

Elizabeth, Richard, Eleanor and Matilda, Buckingham Street, Oldcastle, Britannia. They even named our dog "Harry" and our cat "Camilla." *Geddit?*

Our second name is Pickering. The Pickering coat of arms features an armored helmet and some kind of weird animal with its tongue sticking out. Dad's got it framed on the bathroom wall. Or should I say, in his "throne room."

I found out that the Pickerings originally lived on the side of a hill in Yorkshire, England. We live on the side of a hill in Oldcastle and it all looks like plain old suburbia to me. The only royal view from our house is the London Tavern and drive-thru bottle shop.

But everyone in the suburb of Oldcastle seems to be

in on this bad joke – we've got the Majestic Movieplex, Beefeater Butchery (and its famous "Sandringham" venison sausages), the Lionheart Dry Cleaners, Marquess Mini-mart and the Big-Ears Day Care Centre. Then there's Henry, George and Mary Streets, Edward Court, Charles Drive and Victoria Square. Even at Oldcastle High the sports teams are Wessex, Stuart, Tudor and Saxe-Coburg-Gotha. *Geddit?*

Mostly I don't. What has all this British monarchy stuff got to do with Oldcastle, a million miles away in Australia? I'll bet that the Queen of England hasn't got a corgi called "Pitjanjarra."

When my mother first met Will, she laughed. For her it was one more joke to add to the rest. Prince William. The fact that Will has a full head of hair and the sweetest little sister named Pookie – and neither of them fly helicopters – doesn't seem to matter. The entire Royal Family of Buckingham Street, Oldcastle, thinks my love life is a joke. And, for that matter, so does Bianca.

"When Prince Willy marries Princess Smelly," laughs Bianca, "then you can be the Duke and Duchess of Smelly-Willy."

Sometimes I wish I had a better BF than Bianca.

Which brings me back to the bus. It wasn't till I was getting up from on top of Bianca, mad at myself for spilling pineapple and mint juice on my top, that I realized that my shoulder felt curiously light. There's usually two pounds of stuff hanging off it.

When I realized my handbag was missing, I ran down the aisle waving madly at the bus driver to stop. Too late. We were barreling down the main road by then – trucks and cars on all sides – and before I knew it we were turning off towards Oldcastle. I was totally stressing out. I told Bianca that we should get off at the next stop and wait for the bus to take us back again to look for my bag.

"Your bag has totally been swiped by now, Elly, and your mobile is gone," says Bianca. "It's time you faced facts."

I begged for her mobile to ring the mall and ask if anything had been found and handed in. Then we were at Bianca's stop and she said she couldn't hang around, her mum was expecting her home for lunch (?!) and besides, her phone battery was dead(?!). With that, she was gone, and just as the bus door was closing behind her, I realized that I had no $$$ whatsoever. The only thing I could do was come back here to Buckingham Palace and wait.

Two things occur to me now as I sit in The Dungeon (AKA my bedroom):

1. How come Bianca's phone was dead, when she'd just finished a long convo with Jai and I didn't hear any beeps from the battery winding down?

2. Why was Bianca's mother expecting her home for lunch when everyone knows that Bianca's mother has not prepared a meal, or eaten one, since Bianca was born?

I know the truth. Bianca was rushing off to meet Jai and had care factor zero about my bag and phone. She's right that I have to face facts. And the first major fact is that I really do need a new BF.

Uh-oh! I can hear the Queen Mother walking up the hall and greeting His Excellency the Mutt.

"Here, Harry," she calls. "There you go. Look at you. Good dog."

Then the cat is acknowledged, no doubt with a dismissive, regal wave.

"Camilla! Shoo! Get off that couch. You've left fur all over it."

Then, finally it's my turn.

"Elly. Eleanor. Are you home? I've been trying to call you on your mobile," yells Mum.

All jokes aside, this is going to be right royal torture.

Saturday. 7 p.m.
Seven hours PM.

It's now seven hours since I lost my mobile at the mall and as I predicted, I am dead. Dead to my family. Dead to the world. Dead, as Nan might say, as a doornail.

(BTW: What is a "doornail" anyway and why is it so dead? I Google it and find out that on big doors in medieval times the heavy metal knocker was banged against the head of a nail. Banged so often that the head of the nail was probably as dead as.)

:'-(

I'm in my dungeon feeling as if my head has been banged repeatedly. They all lined up to have a go. The first blow came from my mother.

"Elly! You are so careless! Stupid!" she yells. "Are you

thinking anything at all? Or is your brain just a few cells held together with lip gloss and nail polish?"

I have to admit that my mother had me there for a moment, because sometimes I wonder the same thing myself. I try to think of things in the correct order, but with so much to think about all at once ("Why am I here?" "Where are my sports socks?") it's easy to be distracted by shiny stuff like lip gloss and nail polish.

My mother is an events organizer – a weddings, parties, anything planner. Her business is called "Regal Events." *Geddit?* She values, above all, punctuality and attention to detail. She wouldn't mind if I ran off to Bali as long as I was at the airport on time, had proper travel insurance and wasn't carrying a pair of nail scissors in my hand luggage.

First she rang to report my phone missing and put a block on the number. (Which of course I would have done if I'd had a phone. *Der!*) Then she herded me into the car and back we went to the mall. Groan!

The first stop was the mall admin office, where she inspected the lost and found shelves. There's actually some really good stuff there: a couple of nice bags, cool sunglasses and about thirty-seven mobile phones – none of them mine. Then she took twenty agonizing minutes to carefully fill out a three-page form to report my handbag missing.

After that she dragged me about forty miles – including back to Tiara and to the Hip Pip juice bar – leaving her business card taped on every cash register and pinned to every notice board she could find (thoughtfully bringing along the tape and pins herself). If nothing else, Mrs. Libby Pickering is sure to be offered the job of CEO of Britannia Mall Crime Stoppers.

Of course there was the expected lecture on the way home about the Days Before Mobile Phones Were Invented. All very fascinating. (YAWN!) Truth is my mother would be dead as a doornail too if she didn't have her mobile. A common exchange heard in the halls of Pickering Palace:

"Rick, have you seen my phone?" My mother tears through the kitchen, her car keys jangling in her hand.

"No. Have you seen my car keys?" My father runs the other way, mobile up to his ear.

"Can I use your mobile to ring mine?"

"Can I use your key to my car?"

"Sure, honey."

"Thanks, sweetie."

Ring ring. Jingle jangle. Kiss kiss. Bye bye. Slam!

When I ask my mother if I can use her phone to ring Bianca and Will, she is, predictably, outraged.

"This is a business phone, Elly," she snaps. "I simply can't have you gossiping away when I need it to be free for important calls."

She then takes a call and gossips away for a good half-hour to some client or other about whether it's possible to make gerberas out of icing sugar and, even if you could, would they be suitable for a christening cake? All very important!

Meanwhile, seven entire hours of a Saturday have gone by and I haven't spoken to Will. In this time Will could have rung to tell me he loves me and then, getting no answer, wondered if my declaration of love for him yesterday was just a whim. As if perhaps the fierce sun on the beach had made me dizzy. He'll take the silence of my phone as evidence that I didn't mean what I said, when, in fact, I have never meant anything more in my entire life.

What is it about Will? Why do I love him? He doesn't say much. But then he doesn't have to. In fact, you can tell what Will is really like by the number of things he doesn't do, including:

- *Blah, blah, blah*, on and on about sports. Paint his face blue to go to a football game or stick a hollowed-out watermelon on his head to watch cricket.
- Repeat stupid jokes he read on the Net or heard on breakfast radio.
- Do bad impersonations of Jack Black, Mike Myers, Ben Stiller, Adam Sandler or any other Hollywood star.
- Walk around with earphones stuck in his ears, humming out of tune and air drumming.
- Sit for hours on end on the couch playing stupid video games.
- Jump on you and lick your face to say "hello."

You'd be right in thinking that only an immature dweeb

would do any of this pathetic stuff. You'd also be right in wondering what kind of girl would have a boyfriend who did. Welcome to Bianca and Jai World.

But before I get distracted by stupid Jai, here's more about wonderful Will. I might be utterly obsessed with hair (I don't know why, I just am) but no one has hair like Will Phillips. In fact, if you stand on the steps of Oldcastle High and look across the quad, it's easy to imagine the heads there as a kind of bumpy landscape. You see spiky peaks of black, then tangled bushes of brown, the odd coppery hill, and then your eye is taken by the sight of blond curls threaded with gold that glint in the sun. It's as if you were looking across the rocky, drab plains of Middle-earth to the shimmering Elven forest of Lothlórien.

That's what I feel like when I stand underneath Will's arm – as if I am being sheltered by the golden bough of a golden tree in a golden wood and I am Arwen Evenstar. *Sigh!*

Will looks like an elf or a water sprite or faerie boy. He is tall and slim and has long, elegant fingers. As I said, he doesn't say much, and doesn't have to, because he is deep.

"It's kind of like I am totally connected to the universe when I'm out there in the ocean," says Will. "Every thing, every place, every person, just slips away and I'm just some random drop of, I dunno ..."

Can you believe he says amazing stuff like that? He plays guitar, watches surfing DVDs and picks up trash on the beach whenever we walk there together, because he really cares about Mother Earth. We sit on the sand and watch the moon come up over the ocean whenever we can. Just him and me … and a giant plastic bag full of old soft drink cans and busted rubber flip-flops.

I hope he does say that he loves me – even if I said it first and put him under pressure.

Sometimes I ask Will if he thinks of me when he's out there surfing and loses his grip on reality.

"Sure I do," says Will. "I use you as a marker to remember where my stuff is. You're my land anchor, Elly. You bring me back to earth."

So, there it is. I'm Will's bridge between nothingness and real life. Without me, he'd be swept out to sea. Sometimes he laughs and calls me his "little leg rope." You might think that's a rude thing to say, but no surfer ever goes out without their leg rope. Without that little length of rubber, their board would smash into the rocks or drift across endless oceans.

I don't surf. I've tried a couple of times and I'm useless. Trying to keep up with Will would be needy and pathetic. I like to swim, but mostly I'd rather sit on the beach with a book.

"What are you reading now, Elly?" smiles Will. "Read me something."

And I do. He shakes out crystal drops from his curls, towels his tanned skin and we lie back in the warm sand and

I read to him.

"That's brilliant, Elly," Will whispers. "You get lost in words the same way I do in the waves. Every time I come back to shore, every time you close the cover of your book, I'll bet we're both asking the same question. *What does it all mean?*"

Tonight in The Dungeon I Google *What does it all mean?* and come up with 56,000,000 results. Doesn't look like anyone has worked it out so far.

The second person to bang the door knocker on my dead head this afternoon was my father. I predicted that he would sigh and shake his head and so it came to pass.

"Oh, Elly. This is the third time you've lost your mobile," he exhales. "I just can't see how we're going to find the money to replace it, what with the Global Financial Crisis and everything."

Dad is a driver for a fleet of courier trucks here in Oldcastle called (wait for it) Ascot Couriers! He works really long hours and keeps saying everyone is worried about losing their jobs, but it seems to me that this so-called Global Financial Crisis hasn't actually reached the Oldcastle part of the globe yet. Everyone is just doing what they always have. In the meantime, the GFC is the best excuse any parent has ever come up with for saying "no." *No, you can't have a sleepover/holiday/birthday party/new shoes/school trip/ concert tickets, etc. etc.*

Taking a look out my window tonight, the line through

the London Tavern's drive-thru bottle shop looks as long as it ever did. Seems as though no one in Oldcastle is saying "no" to another drink.

And what, I have to ask, does the "everything" mean in the phrase "the GFC and *everything*"? What's Dad talking about? The GFC and the fact that Mum is never home to cook his dinner? That my sister's boyfriend has a better car than ours? That Dad's going bald? That our lemon tree's got stink bugs? That the earth's polar ice caps are melting?

Under questioning, Dad has to admit that no one's been laid off at work – yet. But he says it's a question of *what if?*

I Googled that too: *What if?* I came up with 304,000,000 results. Again, no real answers.

What are these mysterious *everythings* and *what ifs* hanging off the end of every sentence, as if everyone's paralyzed by hideous possibilities? OK then, *what if?*

How would it have been if Frodo had said, "No way am I taking the ring to Mount Doom. Not with the orcs *and everything*. I mean, *what if?*"

GRRR! Anyway, then I asked my father if I could borrow his phone to call Bianca and Will.

"I'm on call for work, Elly," he says. "It's only seven hours since you lost your phone. I think you'll survive until you see your mates at school on Monday."

Dad shuffled out of The Dungeon, and then my sister Tilly barged in bringing me a bag of chicken-flavored chips and a Diet Coke (AKA bread and water). She hurled my favorite pink stuffed pig at the wall and put her purple suede boots on my white pillowcase.

"Oooh, El, you know they're not gonna get you a new mobile, don't you?" she smirks. "You're stuffed. You should staple your mobile to your forehead, you lose it so often."

V.v. funny. It's OK for her. She's almost eighteen, in her last year at Oldcastle High, and has a part-time job as a waitress at The Earl Bistro. More than that, her boyfriend Eddie plays football for the Sovereigns and has tons of $$$. (I could point out that they are also both royal names, but frankly, by now, I am over it.) Eddie will buy her a new phone anytime she wants.

"Oh, poor you. You want to borrow my mobile and call Prince Charming?" laughs Tilly.

This one hundred and first joke about my relationship should make me want to ram that stuffed pig down my sister's throat. But instead I am so grateful that I could kiss her. I dial Will's number with nervous, rubbery fingers.

"I'm not able to get to the phone right now, but leave a message," says pre-recorded Will.

I gabble that I don't have my mobile and that he will have to contact me though FacePlace.

Then I ring Bianca. The line's busy. So I text: HLP!No phone.Go FacePlace.LuvU.Me.

"Come on now, hand it over," says Tilly, and I reluctantly give her back her phone. Just the weight of it in my hand made me feel better for a bit.

When she leaves an eerie silence descends on The Dungeon – apart from the muffled sound of Mum and Dad watching some lame TV quiz show in the family room.

Sunday. 11 a.m. PM.

Still nothing from Bianca or Will. I've been sitting at my
computer in The Dungeon, looking at my FacePlace, since
nine o'clock this morning. It's about as busy as Victoria
Square, Oldcastle, at nine o'clock on Easter Monday night,
i.e. it's deserted.

The fact that I was wide awake at 8 a.m. should indicate
how stressed out I am. The only time I wake up this early is
on Christmas morning.

Now, hours later, I've posted and poked everyone I know
and it looks like I am the only human being awake on the
entire planet.

I'm so desperate for human interaction that I have even
replied to a two-month-old post from my cousin Anne in

Toolewong. She wants to know if we might come to visit this Christmas holiday. Groan! Toolewong has won the nation's Most Boring Town Award ten years running.

I wrote back that she and Auntie Margaret should come and stay here with us in Oldcastle. The people who live here might have their strange habits, but at least we're close to the beach. Hammerhead, Wobbegong and Gummy are the names of the most popular beaches in Oldcastle. Yes, another very amusing joke. They're all named after sharks! Sometimes you have to wonder about the founding fathers of Oldcastle and their bent sense of humor.

Like the hilarious idea of putting a huge coal-loading terminal right in the middle of one of the most beautiful stretches of beach in Australia! These days the port takes huge container ships and oil supertankers. The place is always noisy and blazing with lights. Any self-respecting, health-nut shark would have racked off years ago.

But the thing is, once you get away from the port and up on top of Winchester Headland, the wharves could be a million miles away. You can see all the sandy beaches looping in and out for miles to the south, like a petticoat with a trim of frothy white lacy surf. It's so, so pretty and when I stand up there on a sunny day I think that Oldcastle is the best place to live in the whole world.

That's where I first kissed Will – on Winchester Headland. He usually stands there with his slick black wetsuit rolled down to his waist, his board under his arm, shading his eyes against the sun. Searching for a wave. This pose is now so familiar to me because Will is always on a hill or a rock or a roof looking out to sea. And if he's not there, he's in or under the water. If it wasn't for me his feet would hardly touch the ground.

Maybe he's not an elf or a water sprite. Maybe he's an angel.

Whatever he is, he's not talking to me on this sunny Sunday morning. I guess he's gone out for a surf. I need to hear his voice. What did he do last night? Where was he? Who did he see? This blackout is driving me insane.

I haven't been able to call anyone because Dad went out at dawn for a day's fishing with his mates and Mum went to the farmers' market in Victoria Square and they took their phones with them. Tilly's still sleeping and she keeps hers under her pillow. Then I hear the familiar rustle of shopping being dumped on the kitchen counter.

"Elly. Get yourself ready. We're due at Nan's in half an hour!" yells my mother.

I scramble to get dressed and belt down the hall because I know there's something waiting for me at Nan's that will rescue me from the bottom of this dark well – a telephone.

"You got yourself ready quickly this morning," says my mother, as she slams the car door.

I tell her something about looking forward to Nan's roast dinner. How it's great to do something with her and Nan – three generations of the one family enjoying a traditional

29

Sunday meal together. As we drive I lay on the enthusiasm as thick as gravy.

I need to get to that telephone.

"Aren't you gorgeous?" beams Mum. "I've loved my mother's baked potatoes ever since I was tiny!"

And then mother dear starts a lecture on home-cooked food in the Days Before Instant Noodles Were Invented. (YAWN!) Usually on the trip to Nan's I'd have my mobile to get me through.

☹ Im bng hld prisner.

But today I am forced to look out the car window and listen to the radio. (Mum has banned me from listening to my iPod in her exalted presence.) I punch the buttons and accidentally end up hearing the team of so-called comedians on the CASTLEROCK 64.5 FM Sunday breakfast show. It reminds me of that pinhead Jai. And then I realize I'm reminded of Jai because he's ACTUALLY on the radio! *What's he saying?*

"So, Jai from South Oldcastle, we're talking about your best sneaky revenge this morning. What you got for us, bro?" asks the host of the show, the utterly painful Bad Mickey B.

"The revenge is on my girl's best friend," Jai sniggers. "She hates my guts, so I've got a special mirror on my FacePlace called 'bad pictures of Elly' and all my mates log on and have a laugh."

"Ha ha ha! Whoa! Good one! Two tickets to the Majestic

Movieplex and a month's supply of Palatial Pizzas for you, my man."

"Thanks Bad Mickey B. WAY TO GO CASTLEROCK FM!" screeches Jai.

And then it's on to an ad. *Beefeater Bangers – fit for a King!* OMG! OH. EMM. GEE!

I turn to my mother. Did she hear that? That was definitely Jai! He lives in South Oldcastle and that was his dweeby voice. That has to be about ME! *Bad pictures of me?* Where did he get them? I can't believe it. My mind goes into total panic. I can't remember Jai ever taking any pictures of me.

Unless he got them from Bianca! From Bianca's phone. We're always mucking around taking stupid pictures of each other on our phones. I've got one of her in a bikini we made out of silverbeet leaves. She's got one of me with a yellow rubber glove on my head, looking like some demented chicken. That hideously embarrassing photo couldn't be up there for the world to see ... COULD IT?

Yes it could. I wouldn't put anything past that weasel Jai. I've never thought he was good enough for Bianca, and I've told her so. She hated me telling her, of course, but it was for her own benefit.

I yell at my mother to turn the car around. I have to get home and get on FacePlace. RIGHT NOW!

"I am not turning around, Nan's expecting us," Mum says calmly. "And if there are silly pictures of you on the

Internet then it's a lesson to you. All this technology you love so much is wonderful, but it also has its downside. You have to realize that it brings good and bad things into your life. Maybe you should just turn off your computer."

I want to yell at her, *WHAT? What are you talking about?* If my mother didn't have her laptop and mobile, Regal Events would be dead and finished inside a week. *She cannot be serious!*

She, of all people, should understand how bad this could be. Libby Pickering is the sort of woman who goes through our digital camera and erases every single picture of her that makes her look fat, or old or even a bit squinty. (Once we went to Bali for ten days and there were only two pictures left after she'd gotten to the camera – even then, she was mostly hidden behind a coconut palm.) When she has finally uploaded the photos she approves of, she edits them to blur out her wrinkles and remove the red-eye. And this is for photos only the family will ever see! Not for totally excruciating shots that could be seen by THE ENTIRE WORLD! Aaargh!

I have to ring Bianca. I beg my mother for her mobile.

"Not while I'm driving. You know we have a rule about taking calls in the car. It's just rude to be prattling on and ignoring your fellow passengers."

She is not a "fellow passenger." She is my mother. She's driving, but I know for a fact she can drive and listen to me talk at the same time. My mother is the Queen of Multi-

Tasking. She could perform brain transplant surgery, launch the Space Shuttle, fold table napkins, head peace talks in the Middle East and make spaghetti bolognese all at the same time. Except when it suits her. Then it's: *Please be quiet, Elly. I'm trying to think.*

Doesn't she realize THIS IS AN EMERGENCY?! I seriously consider jumping out of the moving car and then, mercifully, I see we have pulled up outside Nan's house. I hurtle up the steps and Nan's already standing at the front door.

"Eleanor!" exclaims Nan. "Aren't you looking beautiful this morning. Come in, darling, come in."

I kiss Nan's cheek and speedily admire the vase of pink hydrangeas on the hall stand. Then I edge past her to the oak dresser in the sitting room and grab the phone. I dial Bianca's number (which takes ages because Nan's still got one of those prehistoric telephones with the holes for your fingers. The kind you see on *Antiques Roadshow*).

"Hey, what's happening?" yawns Bianca, even though it's now midday.

I put Bianca through the full interrogation. Has she ever shown Jai the pictures of me on her phone? Has she ever let Jai upload pictures from her phone onto his computer? Does she know he's got this hideous mirror on FacePlace? Is it about me? Has she ever seen it? Who else knows it's there? Did she hear Jai on the radio?

"Really? A month's supply of Palatial Pizzas!" gasps

Bianca. "We better not talk too long, he's probably trying to ring me."

After more intense questioning Bianca admits:

- Yes, she did let Jai see the pics on her phone.
- Yes, she did lend him her phone last week after his got run over by the school bus – but only for a day until he got a new one.
- No, she didn't know his FacePlace mirror had the pics on it.

Then I wait until she gets out of bed, boots up, logs on and ...

"You don't have to worry, El. They're cute," giggles Bianca. "The one of you sticking out your tongue with the chili prawn on it is hilarious! And this one of you in the shower cap! You look like a button mushroom!"

I tell her down the phone, as loudly as I dare, that the entire population of Oldcastle, Britannia, New South Wales, Australia and The Planet Earth is now viewing these pictures of me and thinking I am the Dork of the Universe! WHAT IF WILL SEES THEM?

There is a silence during which I think I can hear Bianca scratching her head and then I hear a *ding* on her computer and I'll bet it's someone posting on her FacePlace mirror saying something like: *Hey, check out Elly Pickering looking like a fungus!*

"Do you think the free pizzas will include the cheesy crust

ones, or just the plain crusts?" asks Bianca.

There's one thing that I've come to appreciate about Nan's ancient phone: You can bang down the handset really hard in someone's ear. It's much more satisfying than pressing a red button. I start to dial Will's number when I hear yelling from the kitchen.

"Eleanor! Come and speak to your grandmother," calls Mum. "We didn't drive all the way over here just so you could run up her phone bill."

I'm going to pretend I didn't hear that because I have to talk to Will. My mother will have to pry this phone out of my cold, dead hands.

"Hey, Elly? What's up? I'm down the coast with my dad this weekend," says Will.

Phew! His dad won't have turned on the radio. They will have listened to Jack Johnson CDs in the car. Will sounds lazy and relaxed. I can tell by his voice that he's been for a surf. I could tell him about everything happening back here in Oldcastle and the exploding supernova disaster in cyberspace, but I hear his voice and none of it seems to matter. It's like the cool incoming tide that sweeps the sand smooth again at the end of a crowded day on Wobbegong Beach.

Instead I just tell him how I'm without a phone now and I'm not sure when I'll be getting a new one.

"That's no biggie. I'll see you at school tomorrow," says Will. "Anyway, you know I'm not much good on the phone. I like seeing your beautiful face when I talk to you."

And I am imagining Will's face now – his suntanned cheeks sparkling with diamonds of dried salt. His dazzling white teeth and wide smile. His soft gray eyes and those long black eyelashes – maybe still glistening wet. I imagine the sun on his curls picking out threads of pure spun gold.

"Well, I better go, but I'm glad you rang," says Will. "I just wanted to say ..."

I finish the sentence for him in my head: *I love you Elly, with all my heart and soul.*

"... that it's good to hear your voice. Don't forget, you're the one that keeps me paddling back to shore."

And then he's gone and I think that maybe he did just tell me, in his own way, that he loves me! And it's like I've bobbed to the surface again and I'm floating on a piece of driftwood in a warm and endless sea.

:'-) Sigh!

After a while the smell of roast beef, Yorkshire pudding and baked potatoes sends me paddling towards Nan's dining room.

Sunday. 5 p.m. PM.

We're driving back home after a really good afternoon at Nan's (considering). We looked through one of her old photograph albums. It was fun to sit around the table and turn the heavy pages, peel back the tissue paper and watch Nan swat at startled silverfish.

There were some hilarious photos of Mum in there from when she was little. My favorite was of her covered from head to toe in white powder after she had upended the flour canister on her head. You could just see her eyes looking like two little dark brown crinkled raisins. There were some real shockers from when she was fifteen, the same age as me. In one she was wearing this fluorescent blue lamé minidress, silver disco tights and white high-heeled ankle boots. She was wearing some kooky black bandanna around her forehead and her hair was sticking up in gelled-back clumps – like she'd tied an electrified cat on her head. HA HA HAH!

My mum was covering her face in her hands and squealing at Nan.

"Stop it, Mum, stop it!"

But Nan just kept turning the pages and embarrassing her.

"And, Elly, this one's of your mother when she was seventeen. She tried to dye her hair blonde with peroxide and it went bright orange like a mandarin."

Nan turned the album so I could examine the pic closely and when I burst out laughing, Nan's shoulders shook so hard with stifled giggling that one of her gold clip-on earrings fell off. Mum and I dived under the table to look for it. We bumped heads and Mum started laughing too.

I suppose it's easy to have a laugh when your life's most embarrassing moments are hidden away in an album in a cupboard and only looked at by silverfish. I wonder what Mum would think if that revolting picture of her and her citrus fruit head was out in the open for all to see.

Still, it was good to see my lovely Nan. It's her seventieth birthday soon, and she said she wants a quiet dinner party with just the family. She reckons she hasn't felt like celebrating much since Pop died two years ago. I hugged her when she said that. She tries not to show it, but I know she misses Pop. You can tell from their wedding photos how much she loved him. Even from black-and-white photos taken in 1959, you can tell.

"Nonsense, Mum, you have to have a party!" my mother nags. (She would nag the Prime Minister, I tell you.) "It's a big milestone. You have to celebrate. Eugenie's restaurant would be perfect. Marg can bring the mob down from Toolewong. All your ladies from the card club can come, and all Dad's old friends from work."

"I'm not sure I still have all their addresses," says Nan.

"Don't worry, I'll track them down on the Net," Mum replies.

"With a net?"

"No, Mum! On the *Internet!*"

"Well, I'm sure you won't find them that way," Nan shakes her head. "They don't have computers and things. Some of them might be in the phone book I suppose. Maybe if I hunt out one of my old Christmas card lists."

Things have sure changed since Nan's day. She told me that her grandad's house was one of the first in Oldcastle to get a telephone. It was a "party line" – where anyone could listen in to your private conversations! Imagine that!

But then again, FacePlace isn't that much different. Unless you put your page on the highest security, anyone can drop in and read the postings on your mirror. So you have to be really careful what you say on there. But the good thing is, if I wanted to invite my friends to a party I could send out one instantaneous message to all 105 of them – although you'd have to be careful 500 people didn't turn up. (Probably not the Prime Minister.)

Thinking of FacePlace and my missing mobile, I felt sick. I had to get home and see what had happened while I was out of range at Nan's. And soon enough Mum's event planner mind was back in action and she was heading for the door and dialing her mobile at the same time. Even as Nan was waving us off, Mum was getting advice on party flowers from her best friend Tina, who owns the Diana's Bouquet florist.

Now we're almost home and she has talked the whole time! I suppose it would be a waste of breath to remind her of what she said on the way to Nan's – that it's rude to prattle on the phone and ignore your fellow passengers. My mother thinks that when I talk on the phone it's just dumb gossip and when she talks it's high-powered business negotiations. Now Mum's yakking about Tina's new bedroom wallpaper (orchids or birds of paradise?). I'd like to know what that's got to do with high-powered business.

When Mum finally hangs up, I ask her about getting a new mobile. I tell her it's *vital* that I get one.

"Well, you should have thought of that before you lost it," says my brainiac mother.

Yeah, the same way she should think about how much she needs her reading glasses before she loses them. It's an excruciating piece of mother logic and reminds me of what she always says: *If it looks like you're going to be late, Eleanor, come home early.* Der!

"Money's really tight this year, what with the Global

Financial Crisis and *everything*," Mum continues.

It's exactly what Dad said! Do they get together and learn this stuff off a script? Then I do the "personal safety" speech, reminding her that the mobile isn't just for my benefit. It's also so that she knows where I am at all times and she can speak to me whenever she wants.

"You'll just have to use a pay phone," she counters.

I point out that the only working pay phone in Oldcastle is the one they use to call taxis outside the London Tavern. Does she really want me hanging out there?

If I am abducted by some weird cult she will be really sorry she didn't get me a new mobile. I won't be able to stop and call her from a public telephone when I'm bound and gagged in the back of a minivan speeding up the highway.

Mum laughs at this. She actually laughs! And then I make the point that I need to speak to my friends. How will I do that without a mobile?

"When I was a girl, we wrote letters or just made appointments to meet up and kept them. Somehow I managed to have a social life," she says. "Besides, you still have your computer and you can borrow Tilly's phone."

Wrote letters? Made appointments? *Is she insane?* And as for borrowing Tilly's phone – how will I do that when it's already in use 24/7? And yes, I can use my computer, but everyone texts these days. That's just the way it is.

:-> AAMOF

Then I have to endure Part II of the lecture on the Days

41

Before Mobile Phones Were Invented. Does this make any sense to anyone? I mean, how far do we want to go with this logic? Back to the days before the invention of the actual telephone, the television, the car, the steam train ... the wheel? Was there some Neanderthal cave mother lecturing her daughter about the Days Before Fire Was Invented. *We had to eat everything raw, and a good thing too!*

After listening to her rave on about how she used to take personal responsibility for her whereabouts *blah, blah, blah*, I make the big offer to pay for a new mobile myself.

"Well, Elly," she says, "if you can find a part-time job and save up, you can get a new mobile, but from what I see, money burns a hole in your pocket. And it will certainly mean you'll be spending a whole lot less time down at the beach with Will. Think about that."

Gee, Mum, that's encouraging. But she does make me think. What sort of part-time jobs are available in Oldcastle? With this GFC *and everything* it's not going to be that easy to find one. And OK, it might mean less time with Will, but then again, just being able to hear his voice whenever I want ... that has to be worth it. Without my mobile, how will we ever make time to be together?

Then there's the matter of keeping up with my so-called BF, Bianca.

How did I end up with a B-grade BF like Bianca? She came to me second-hand, along with a surfboard, wetsuit and a collection of pig ornaments. My *real* best friend

Carmelita left Oldcastle last year. I've known her since the first day I went to Big-Ears Day Care Centre and she took a nap next to me clutching her blankie. Her family went macadamia nut farming in Queensland. Now we talk to each other mostly via FacePlace. I miss her so much.

M$ULKECRZ

When she left she gave me her board and wetsuit, because all the beaches near the farm are fringed with mangrove flats and there's no surf. She also left me her pig collection. How she started collecting pigs is sort of a strange story. Her parents are Spanish. Her full name is Carmelita Consuela Martinez. Her dad is obsessed with eating pigs – bacon, prosciutto, chorizo, cured jamón, pork scratchings, pork sausages and (erk!) trotters. He feasts on pigs at almost every meal.

Anyway, one day Carmelita saw this documentary on TV about battery farm pigs and was so upset to see them caged like that that she became a vegetarian. She joined FAP (Free All Pigs) and started to collect all manner of porkers – ceramic, pottery, plush, plastic and stuffed – and ended up with 357 of them! When the family moved to Queensland, her dad promised she could have a real, live, free-range pig of her own that could spend its natural life without fear of being eaten. She named it Viscount (some Oldcastle traditions never leave you, it seems). She passed her pig collection on to me and I have it displayed on a wall unit in The Dungeon. I keep one special stuffed pink pig on my bed to remind me of her.

43

Sometimes I think that the other pig she gave me was Bianca. Bianca Ponsford moved next door to Carmelita in East Oldcastle about three years ago and wound up in the same year as us at Oldcastle High. The Martinez, Ponsford and Pickering parents somehow became best friends, so that meant we ended up hanging out a lot together. When Carmelita left, I guess Bianca and I just became closer through mutual grief and loneliness. The thing is that Bianca and I are like oil and water and Carmelita was like ... er ... detergent. She dissolved our differences and, in the end, we made a really good girlfriend combo.

Bianca was the wild one who dared us to do all the things we were too scared to do − like the day we hid in the old World War II fortifications on Winchester Headland and dropped water bombs on the bushwalkers below.

Carmelita was the sunny one who always made us feel like we were in a Bollywood musical − we danced down the escalators in Britannia Mall and reenacted wet sari scenes wading through the fountain in Victoria Square.

I was the shy one who was always asking the Big Questions − we held a séance in Oldcastle Cemetery on Halloween and talked Secret Women's Business in the dark caves at the end of Gummy Beach below the Aboriginal rock carvings.

Now Carmelita's not here and sometimes when I'm with Bianca I think we should call Greenpeace. Total oil spill disaster zone!

We were just working it out and getting a lot closer

when Bianca got together with Jai and I got together with Will. If we are like oil and water, then Jai and Will are night and day. There is nothing I can think of that will ever make them see the world in the same light. Jai calls Will "that seaweed head" and Will calls Jai "the redneck." The one time we went on a double date, Jai ended up tipping a lime slushie on Will's back and Will whacked Jai on the bridge of the nose with the rail of his board.

Since then Bianca and I have made a pact never to put our boyfriends together. And while we are still BFs, it seems that the older we get, the more we are drifting apart. I guess we're still clinging to each other because we don't know what comes next. If we listen to our boyfriends and never see each other, what then? Who will tell me it's time to trash my Disney Princess undies? Who will art-direct Bianca's hair and do tech support on her laptop?

Mum negotiates the car down the driveway at Buckingham Palace and, as usual, parks the passenger-side door smack into the hedge.

"Come on, Elly," she yells. "Grab that package of Nan's leftover dessert off the back seat and come inside. You have to get your uniform ready for tomorrow."

Oh good, thanks for the reminder. 'Cos I was thinking of going to school in the nude!

Sunday. 9 p.m. PM.

I have calculated that it's now thirty-three hours since I lost my mobile phone. This means it has been gone 2,040 minutes, which is a shame because I could have used at least 2,000 of those minutes to abuse Bianca Ponsford.

As soon as I got home I raced to The Dungeon and logged on to my computer. There was an eye2eye from Carmelita (and we only use eye2eye when it's strictly just between us). One part stood out: *Just saw Jai's FacePlace! How did he get those pics? What's the deal?*

That nails it. She wouldn't usually bother to look on Jai's FacePlace. The only way Carmelita, now living on a macadamia nut farm in Queensland with a free-range pig and surrounded by mangrove swamp, would have known about those pictures is if Bianca had told her!

I went to Jai's page and had a look at the entire horror show. There are ten pics – including the unfortunate rubber glove chicken and mushroom-head shots and the chili-prawn-tongue portrait. They are (in no particular order of grossness):

- Me asleep on the beach with dribble coming out of my mouth.
- Me in a low-fat yogurt face pack with slices of cucumber on my eyes.
- Me with my hair over my face looking like a yeti.
- Me going cross-eyed and "smoking" a piece of celery.
- Me kissing my pink stuffed pig.
- Me inside a sleeping bag impersonating a giant plaid maggot.
- Me standing on the bench of the bus stop and pretending to be Beyoncé, using my hairbrush as a microphone.

If a stranger just dropped in to Jai's FacePlace site and looked at these photos, they would have to wonder why this person "Elly" hadn't already curled up and died from acute embarrassment hemorrhage. I wonder myself as I look at Jai's profile pic. He looks as nauseatingly smug as a fresh custard tart from the Duchess Bakery.

I read some of the comments people have left on Jai's mirror. Most of them are anonymous, which is typical.

Ha ha ha!

Doesn't she know smoking is bad for you? Try to stop that celery habit, babe.

ROFL

Cluck cluck cluck! Wot a chick!

Elly is hot. Wish I was that pink pig! SWALK!

WLUMRYME?

Will's dating a sheepdog. LOL

Elly's smokin celery
Pashin on a pig
Makin like Beyoncé
Wearin a bad wig.
Heh!
The Phantom Rhymer!

GRRR! This is so not fair! I am tempted to scrawl all kinds of insulting stuff on Jai's mirror, but I know he'd really enjoy that in his own warped way. If I had my phone I could post some equally hideous pictures of him. (I'm sure I have one of him with a cucumber down his football shorts!) But there is probably someone, somewhere, right this minute, erasing them forever.

I am just thinking of all kinds of payback schemes, starting with Jai's head and a handful of darts, when I hear the front door slam. It must be Dad, finally back from his fishing trip. I head up the hall, but halfway I hear that an argument has already started.

"Look at the time! You could have rung me, Rick," accuses my mother.

"Well, I've been trying, but you're never off the phone," Dad complains.

"You could have sent me a text or rung on Elly's phone ... oh." She falters as she remembers the awful truth.

I stop and listen as I hear a wet fish slapped on the kitchen counter.

"Six whiting, a nice size too, and two big snapper," he says, making pathetic dead offerings to calm my mother. "What are we going to do about that girl? This is the third phone she's lost! Her brain's like a sieve. It's not like she's losing a beach towel or a pair of flip-flops. How much did the last one cost?"

"One hundred dollars."

"Well, we just don't have that money right now. I need new tires for my truck, the house insurance is due, then there's the taxes ..."

"Don't, Rick, don't. It just makes me feel depressed. She says she'll get a part-time job and save up, but even if she

49

could find a job ..."

"I'm not keen on her working," says Dad sternly. "Not at her age and without a phone, catching buses all over the place. I'm not happy with that. Maybe for her birthday."

I gasp at this. My birthday? That's months away! I clamp my hand over my mouth to stop from screaming.

"For Christmas. We'll give her one for Christmas. I should get some cash in by then. I've got a couple of big weddings ..."

"Yeah, OK, for Christmas. Although she's not going to be happy."

"She's got to learn the lesson, Rick. But it's going to be a real pain; she's hard enough to track down as it is."

"She'll just have to do things the old-fashioned way and come home when she's told. When I was her age there were no such things as mobile ..."

I turn away and trudge back up the hall. I've already heard Parts I and II of that particular speech and I'm not keen for Part III.

Looking at my calendar now I see that today is the ninth of October and there are seventy-seven days until Christmas. That's seventy-seven whole days – a quick calculation comes up with more than 100,000 minutes! This means I will be uncontactable for the end of school, the beginning of the holidays, the start of summer and all the Christmas parties. (How will Santa find me? Hah!)

But more than that, the Oldcastle High combined Years Eight, Nine and Ten dance is coming up in about ten days.

How am I supposed to get myself organized without a mobile?

Hasn't anyone remembered (hello?) that *we don't have a home phone!* Dad got rid of the landline earlier this year when he looked at the mobile bills coming in and said we couldn't afford the landline as well.

Maybe I should start burning a fire here on the roof of the Palace so I can send smoke signals to my friends? Train a flock of carrier pigeons? Spell out, *meet you at 10 at the mall* in rocks on the front lawn?

I eye2eye Carmelita and tell her the whole, sad story. She writes back, *OMG! What are you going to do about the pics?* I reply that I have no idea.

I Google "unauthorized use of photos on the Net" and come up with 3,120,000 results.

There's no easy way to stop Jai!

I go to a legal aid website and discover that because Bianca took the photos, she owns the copyright and can basically do what she likes with them. How can this be right?

There are apparently four ways I can stop Jai:

1. Get legal advice for defamation action.
I have to prove that by publishing the photos, Jai is exposing me to "hatred, contempt or ridicule" and causing me "to be shunned or avoided." Well, I should have a pretty good case – except that around Oldcastle High most people will be thrilled that Jai's won free

pizzas and think the pics are funny! Also legal advice costs mega $$$.

2. Investigate Trade Practices Act.
Unfortunately I have to prove that the use of my image will "mislead or deceive consumers." Forget this one.

3. Get legal advice for "passing off."
This is going to be hard too. I have to prove that the pics will damage my business reputation – a reputation which I, of course, do not have. I note that it says this law is "of limited use" to the "average person in the street." That, sadly, is me. Again, no use. (Also, see above re: $$$.)

4. Check out "invasion of privacy."
"There is no general right of privacy in Australia."

Whaaa ...? I'll have to wait until I'm eighteen and run for Parliament and get the laws changed. In the meantime it looks like, legally, I just have to suck it up.

So, all this leaves me with no option but to insist that Bianca tell Jai to take the pics down, or else!

Or else ...?

And, thinking about what this "or else" could be, I go to bed and try to get some sleep.

Monday. 2 a.m. PM.

I wake up with a list of "or elses," including Jai's murder, Bianca's assassination, or sweet, sweet revenge. I still have my camera, after all, and getting totally embarrassing photos of Jai shouldn't be that hard. (Given that if he's awake and breathing, he's embarrassing.) Then I can put them up on my FacePlace mirror and invite the world to have a look! I stash my camera in my schoolbag and go back to bed, kiss my stuffed pink pig and dream of Will.

Monday morning.
Two days PM.

I got to school late because I usually set the alarm on my phone. I forgot I didn't have it, totally slept in and missed the bus.

I look across the math classroom now and one of Jai's stupid mates sticks his tongue out at me and goes, "Ow, ow, ow, hot, hot," impersonating me with a chili prawn on my tongue. *Right! That does it!* If one more person mimes me singing into a hairbrush or with my hair over my face and growling like a yeti or "smoking" a pen, I am going to *lose it!* It seems like the whole of Year Nine has checked out Jai's FacePlace.

This sucks, big time!

I'm staring across at Bianca and trying to give her the

evil eye. But this is impossible because today her hair is sort of weirdly teased up at the back like a pot scourer, and the front is hanging down, parted in the middle like a yellow shower curtain and I can't see her eyes. She must know that I am still furious with her. The last time we spoke I slammed Nan's phone down in her ear. She turns, parts her hair a bit and smiles at me. I glare back. By rights, I should never speak to her again.

Except I am reminded of a saying my dad always quotes: "Keep your friends close, and your enemies closer." Some old Chinese warrior said it, apparently. (Although what use this is in Dad's work at Ascot Couriers is a mystery. Shouldn't he be quoting Winston Churchill? "We shall fight on the beaches"? Dad's always coming home with his trousers torn by this huge mixed-breed dog in a house at Gummy Beach.)

So the line from the old Chinese guy means that I should pretend nothing's happened and be really friendly with Bianca. This will put me in a better position to get some truly hideous pics of Jai. I reach down and pat my school bag. The camera's still there, charged and ready to go.

As I'm thinking about all this, I see a pile of golden curls bob past the window on its way to the sports field. It's Will, heading for the field with his mob from Year Ten.

I'll catch him under the jacaranda tree near the back fence at lunch. That's where he goes to chill. Maybe he'll have some ideas for incriminating photographs. If I could possibly get a shot of Jai renting the *Mamma Mia!* DVD his reputation would be toast.

The bell rings and I head for the door. Bianca's peering at me through her hair curtain and shuffling closer. She's looking a bit guilty, which is a start, I suppose. If she was a BF worthy of the title, she would have demanded Jai take down the photos straight away. I am just about to tell her this when I remember the line about keeping your enemies closer.

I give her a kiss and compliment her on her hair. (Liar!)

"Hey, Jell ... er ... I mean, Elly. Love your braids," Bianca beams.

I've worn braids today because I have decided to mount a one-woman campaign to make them fashionable again. With my tanned skin and long brown hair, I look a bit American Indian, which is pretty "on trend" I reckon.

I can't help noticing that Bianca's hair has a slight greenish tinge. She's been spending too much time in her swimming pool again. Her dad's a maniac with the chlorine. He doesn't get the leaves and gunk out, just pours more and more stuff in it till you can taste it. On a hot day it feels like you're swimming in tom yum soup. The chlorine makes the peroxide streaks in Bianca's hair turn sort of moldy. Erk!

I don't say anything about this, of course, and then, just as I am following Bianca down the stairs, Jai jumps in between us.

"We're all going to Palatial Pizzas for our first freebie, you wanna come, Bianca?" he asks. His beady eyes are like two black olive pits. Up close I can see his flaky skin and yellow pimples. He's got a face like a barbecue special, with extra cheese. But then, Bianca must be a meat-lover, 'cos she just nods and giggles.

"So, um, you want to come, Elly?" Bianca asks. "After all, it's 'cos of you that we ... er ..."

Bianca runs out of things to say here. After all, what can she say? *It's 'cos of your humiliation that we can all go and stuff our faces? A free thin-and-crispy crust means more to me than our entire friendship?*

I make some pathetic excuse about having to meet Tilly and then just walk away. I could go and try to get some ugly shots of Jai feeding his face, but now's not the time. He'd know what I was up to. Besides, I don't think I could manage to swallow one bite if I had to look at him. (BTW, up close he smells like an anchovy. Eeeyew!)

"So, I'll save you a piece!" Bianca calls after me.

Yeah, Bianca! Like a piece of cold pizza will somehow make up for all the mortification your jerk boyfriend has caused me! I can feel tears coming and I escape into the bathrooms so no one can see. I'm looking in the mirror and wiping my eyes with a scrap of paper towel when one of the girls from Year Ten starts scoping me out.

"Hey, Pickering! Didn't recognize you without that shower cap on your head," says the blob with mouse-brown frizz on top.

I am just about to have a complete nervous breakdown

when I hear a cubicle door open behind me.

"Rack off, you freak!" yells Tilly.

"You're a pair of pickled … *losers!*" Furball replies, and then makes a fast escape.

So lame! Pickled onion, pickled herring, pick-yourring … I've heard it all before.

Then Tilly turns to me, bottom lip stuck out, her face a perfect portrait of sympathy.

"Hey, Elly," she says. "I've heard what's been happening. It's *so* not fair."

And it's like the dam breaks and I am in Tilly's arms, crying really hard. I hear a few people stick their head in the door and say *uh-oh!* and then leave again. Now the word will get around that Jai has made me cry. That's the last thing I wanted that lowlife to know and I cry even harder.

"You know what, Els? I've got a good idea," says Tilly.

And I can hear from the tone of her voice that it is a good idea. I hope it's one of Tilly's award-winning, good ideas.

Tilly is one clever gal. She's brilliant at math and science. She's a champion swimmer and plays the flute. Not only that, she is quite beautiful. (This happened only recently when she suddenly grew these amazing long legs and had her braces removed.) She has white skin, but perfectly straight chocolate brown hair and greenish eyes, like me. Only her eyes are an elegant almond shape, where mine are round, like walnuts. With all this you'd think she would be utterly graceful and kind to all, but she does have an evil streak in her. Sometimes she uses her dark arts on me, but mostly we're cool.

"That Jai is a serial pest," says Tilly, her eyes narrowing. She pauses and I can almost hear her thinking.

"What we need are some classic pics of him to use for our own evil purposes."

I stop sniffling. That's exactly what I was thinking!

"We are sisters after all, El. Let's face it, you can't go through life with a chronic name like Pickering and not develop a few revenge strategies. When we get home tonight we'll get down to business. Until then, just stay clear of him. And by the way, you have snot coming out your nose."

Tilly leans in to the mirror and applies balm to her pretty lips (she's addicted to the stuff) while I mop up my watery snot. Then she smacks a kiss at me and leaves. I head off to find sanctuary with Will under the jacaranda tree.

I find Will alone, kicking back, lying on the grass and looking at the sky through the branches. I resist the urge to ask him, *what are you thinking?* I've asked him this before and usually his reply doesn't make much sense: *Nothing. Everything. Just random disconnected stuff. That's where you find the truth.* (Huh?)

As I suspected, he hasn't seen the pics. Will hardly ever goes on FacePlace. They've only got one laptop at his house and his mum Jasmine uses it most of the time. The Phillips family live right on the beach at Hammerhead. I love their house. It's an old wooden shack, jammed full of Jasmine's watercolors and pottery. There are surfboards stacked in every corner and more still are piled up on the roof beams with the Tibetan prayer flags, driftwood and crusty old lanterns covered in shells and dried barnacles.

His dad Took (that's his nickname, I think his real name's Greg) is a full-on old surf rat greenie. He's always ranting about how much he hates computers and mobile phones – all the "techno-horrors," he calls them.

"They make the world move too fast," says Took. "They're like a rope around your neck. People reckon they can ring you anytime they like or send you some dopey email or message and tell you what's on their mind. If they just sat and thought about it for a minute, they wouldn't be spouting such nonstop garbage!

"Those idiots out in West Britannia use their technology to get these tiny pictures of the surf sent to 'em on their mobile phones. Pictures big as a postage stamp! What's that about? And then, if there are any waves, they come in droves down here and hassle the locals. There's no respect for the surf life anymore. I live here on the beach where I can smell and see and hear the ocean, be part of it all. That's what it's about."

When he gets on one of his raves, it can go on for hours ...

"There are three million computers sold in this country every year. The greedy leeches suck down fossil fuels and most of 'em end up in landfills where all the filthy chemicals inside all that shiny new metal and plastic – mercury, barium, flame retardants, lead, chromium and cadmium – get into the waterways and kill fish and birds. I'd ban computers. And mobile phones. Every last one of 'em.

"When I was a kid ..."

Sometimes, though, Will gets to go on his mum's computer and check out the surf sites. He has got a mobile, but I don't think Took even knows the number.

I sit on the grass next to Will and tell the whole story about what's on the Net and he stands up and tears at his tie. He paces the grass. I can see that he's mad and I'm grateful.

"Why do you even look at this stuff, Elly?" Will says. "Dad's right. It's all bogus! You want me to pay out on that redneck?" he asks fiercely.

I just smile like a cat and tell Will that I already have a payback in mind for Jai and he grins back at me.

"Sweet! I knew you would. That's what I like about you, Elly, you're strong and independent. Most chicks would go into total meltdown over something like this. And what you have to remember is that anything that's said about you in cyberspace isn't really real. It's like, in another universe."

There's one thing in this speech that makes me take notice. *That's what I like about you.* Why didn't Will say, *that's what I LOVE about you.* Still, anything Will says makes my insides melt and go gooey until I'm a soft-center caramel. He could read from the Oldcastle Yellow Pages and I would be standing there looking at him like that dopey Puss in Boots from *Shrek*.

And then he leans in and kisses me and I see the golden light shifting through the golden branches above and it occurs to me that as long as Will wants to kiss me, it doesn't matter what the world says. And then I think of Jai again and it's like a nasty orc is peering at me from behind a tree in Lothlórien.

"Hey, where's your ring?" says Will, noticing the bare finger on the hand I place on his warm chest.

The magic spell is broken. I have to admit that I've lost the friendship ring he gave me – the darling silver one with the tiny blue stones.

"Elly!" he moans. "That ring cost me heaps! I had to work at the surf shop for six Saturday mornings straight to get the money for that ring! You should have been more careful if you knew you were gonna just lose it."

I can't believe he's sounding just like my mother and father! OK, so I lost my mobile. I lost my handbag. I lost the ring. But it's as if they're more important than me in person. It's only "stuff" after all. Stuff's always getting lost. Why doesn't anyone ever think about all the stuff they've *found?* Sometimes it seems like people value stuff more than actual, breathing human beings.

I wonder if things go missing for a reason. As if by their absence, they might be trying to tell you something. To make you see life in a new way. Then I think of my lost friendship ring and I wonder what that means for Will and me?

I hate thinking stuff like this!

The bell rings and Will and I trudge back across to class, not looking at each other.

Monday night.
Two days PM.

"So, here's the plan," says Tilly, in between blowing on ten perfectly painted purple fingernails.

She leans over the pile of junk on her unmade bed in the South Wing of Buckingham Palace and looks me straight in the eye.

"I happen to know for a fact that Jai is always making moves on Lily Cameron from Year Twelve. Georgie Daniels told me."

I gasp, even though I wouldn't put anything past Jai. Does Bianca know about this? If she did, she would be devastated.

"We all have a good laugh about it," Tilly giggles and wiggles, swishing her hair over her shoulders. "Lily goes out with Jai's older brother Jayden, right? So she's over at his house a lot. Every time Jayden's not looking, Jai's showing off in front of Lily – bombing her in the pool or parading around in his bathing suit and showing off his weedy body. She said he's even asked her out! Even though he's two years younger. Can you ever imagine a Year Twelve girl going for someone like Jai? It's so *utterly* pathetic!"

I can't help feeling sorry for Bianca. If Will ever did that behind my back ...!

"So this is what we do. We have to get Jai in some sort of compromising position with Lily – without Bianca or Jayden knowing. I snap away and then post the photos. *Lah de dee, la de dah!*" Tilly clicks her fingers in front of my nose. "No more Jai and Bianca. And of course, Jayden will be totally furious! He'll want to kill Jai! That should teach him a lesson."

I'm not feeling entirely comfortable with this. Apart from not particularly wanting to break up Jai and Bianca, I'm not even sure it's legal.

I tell Tilly that I think this is called "entrapment" and lean over to Google it on her laptop. I find 2,610,000 results.

Entrapment is the inducing, by a law enforcer, of a person to commit a crime which ordinarily they may not have been likely to commit. In some circumstances entrapment may serve as a defense against criminal guilt.

"That's what Bianca and Jai did to you! OK, they're not law

enforcers – but apart from that, it's exactly the same," Tilly continues. "You were making an idiot of yourself …"

I wasn't making an "idiot" of myself. I was just having fun. It was supposed to be private. I never thought for a moment that the pictures Bianca took would end up *on the Net*!

"… and all of a sudden there's a camera in your face," says Tilly.

She's right. There was that bloke who plays football for the Sovereigns who came out of the London Tavern drunk. Some girls followed him and filmed him on their mobiles and that footage ended up on the TV news! Like Tilly's boyfriend Eddie says – there are cameras everywhere these days. Soon everyone will have to have an extreme makeover just to go down to the shops.

"I reckon what happened to you sounds like 'entrapment,' don't you?" argues Tilly.

I have to nod that it does, but I can't believe Bianca did it on purpose. She's usually guilty of being brainless more than anything else. Why would she want to humiliate me?

"You know what I reckon, Els?" says Tilly, as she slumps back on her bed and attacks herself with lip balm (again). "I reckon Jai and Bianca did it so that Will would see the photos and then dump you."

I'm shocked! Well, I suspected this, but to hear it out of someone else's mouth! Could Bianca really be that calculating?

"Bianca's a blonde bimbo and she's totally jealous of you. Anyone can see that," Tilly snorts.

If this is what Jai and Bianca had in mind then it WON'T WORK! Even if Will did see those dumb shots, he wouldn't care! Our relationship is stronger than that.

Now I'm angry!

"The thing is," says Tilly, "all the girls at Oldcastle adore Will and all the boys want to be like him. And you're the one that got him. You're pretty, and intelligent. You two are like this perfect, golden couple."

I have to smile. That's what it feels like when I'm with Will.

"So, of course everyone wants to break you up! People hate perfection. It just makes them feel inadequate. And that bully Jai is leading the way."

Well, if that's what they really want, I'll never give them the satisfaction. I tune in to all the details of Tilly's plan and I have to say, it's perfectly evil! Bring it on!

Back in The Dungeon I'm tempted to go on Jai's FacePlace again and see if anyone else has had anything rude to say about me. But I manage to hold back from torturing myself one more time. Like Will says, anything that's on there's not really real.

Instead, something Tilly said about Jai being a bully makes me think and I Google "cyberbullying." There are 1,130,000 results.

Cyberbullying is when one or many people use technology such as the Internet, mobile telephones or other electronic devices, to mock, embarrass, insult or defame another person or persons.

That's EXACTLY what's happening to me! So what should I do? There's plenty of advice here.

- **Tell your parents.**

I did that already and what did Mum say? "Turn the computer off."

- **Tell your teachers.**

Hah! Like the crocks at Oldcastle High would take me seriously! My English teacher, Mr. York, is the only one who's got a FacePlace site and there are these pathetic pictures of his sad model trains on it! Like Mum, the teachers would just say "put down your mouse and walk away."

BTW: Isn't it weird that all the advice about how to deal with cyberbullies tells you to turn off the computer – but if you didn't have your computer, where would you go for advice?

I don't know what I'd do without the Internet. Being without my mobile is bad enough ... *but the Net?*

Don't even talk about it!

I search around a bit more and there is one paragraph here that catches my eye: *Like drinking and driving, the Internet and emotions should never be mixed. Don't react or you could end up being a cyberbully yourself.*

Is that what Tilly's plan might do? Turn me into a

cyberbully and escalate this whole thing into World War III? Still, I can't be a wimp about it – Jai started it so he will get what he deserves! If he feels inadequate now, wait till I get through with him. He'll be lower than a snake's armpit.

Friday afternoon.
Six days PM.

It's been the longest and boringest week of my entire life. The weather in Oldcastle has been really bad – rainy and windy. It should be spring, but this October week feels more like winter. At least I know that I haven't missed a thing without my mobile, because there's been nothing to miss.

I spent a lot of time this week in The Dungeon working on the latest edition of the school newsletter. This is my first year as Editor-in-Chief. I like being the boss, even though I only have a staff of one – Karen Crenshaw, who does all the design. When Mr. York gave me the editorship, the first thing I did was change the name from *Ye Olde Castle News* (!) to the *Posh Post*. (You know – after Victoria Beckham, AKA Posh Spice, who's modern English royalty. *Geddit?*)

Well at least it's a *new* joke. Even if sometimes I think there's nothing new about Oldcastle.

Seriously, *Ye Olde Castle News* was ye olde rag! There has to be more to life at Oldcastle High than the usual brain-numbing reports from school trips and the sports results: *Once again the senior football team showed they were the equal to any school in the Britannia District League with a convincing win over Lady Jane Selective High.*

The next thing I did was take the newsletter online, which made it so much more eco-friendly. The old printed newsletter was just another thing to chuck away. So now the *Posh Post* comes out every month at www.poshpost.oh.au. It's got heaps of good stuff on it – links to other websites, photo galleries, articles, cartoons. I've made a page for book, movie and television reviews. There's also a gallery for celebrity sightings (unfortunately that idiot Bad Mickey B's on there) and it's where I was going to post the pic of Bianca and Hugh Jackman – the pic which is now (shudder) gone forever!

I took the pic on the red carpet at the Majestic Movieplex premiere of *Australia* last year. Bianca's leaning over the railing as Hugh's walking past and you can see half of her face behind his left shoulder. It's the first and only time I can remember any real celebrity visiting Oldcastle, so I can understand why Bianca's so dark at me for losing it.

Anyone can post comments on the *Posh Post* site if they want, although I get to choose what goes up, 'cos I'm the webmaster. But so far most comments, apart from the insulting anonymous ones, are tedious letters from teachers. I *have* to use them. *Sigh!* So the *Posh Post* is a lot more dreary than I'd like it to be. The students around here don't seem to care much about what goes on the site, but I do. I'd like to be a journalist one day and Mr. York says he'll count my work on the *Posh Post* as part of my exam results.

"You're quite a tidy writer with a very entertaining turn of phrase," says Mr. York, as he scrolls the pages. "I certainly think we'll be seeing the name Elly Pickering in the media in the future."

Only thing is, he fancies that I will be reporting from a war zone in the Middle East and I'd like to be a fashion writer. Not that reporting on fashion around here has much of a future: *This sizzling summer in Oldcastle the hot look is T-shirts, tank tops, cargo pants and rubber flip-flops – the same as it was last season … and the one before that.*

Since I came home from school I've been putting together a photo gallery of the school senior football final. (OK, there are some things I *have* to do, but at least it's a fun slideshow with some music behind it.)

It's also been a lonely week because I'm still avoiding Bianca. That's been easier without my mobile. The hideous pics of me were still in Jai's great photograph album in cyberspace the last time I looked. Which is making me madder and madder. I can only think that Tilly's absolutely right and that Bianca is being jealous and destructive. All Bianca has to do is the right thing. As soon as Jai takes the stupid pics down, I will call off Tilly the attack corgi.

The other downer is that I haven't been able to talk to Will. He's been away from school on some surf camp with the Year Ten boys all week. At least I know he still won't have seen the pics Jai put up, 'cos it's strictly "no computers" at school camps, and Will's even less interested in looking at FacePlace on people's phones than he is on a computer.

It's been driving me crazy not to hear his voice. I've been spending hours looking at a photo gallery I made of him – Will lying in the sand, his golden hair tangled in seaweed; Will's great big feet crusted with pearly shells; Will way out the back suspended in a blue, blue ocean, sitting on his board and waving to me. Honestly, he is the most gorgeous boy in the world! Maybe he's not an elf or a faerie or an angel. Maybe he's a merman.

LUWAMH XXXX

Tilly's putting her plan into action tonight. Lily Cameron has told her boyfriend Jayden that she's having a "girls' night in" and can't see him. Then she's going to ring Jai and ask him to drop by her house with a couple of free Palatial Pizzas. Tilly will be there with her camera and try to get Jai into the spa with Lily. Then she'll snap away! Tilly says Lily's only too happy to put them on her FacePlace mirror and then …

ROFL

It'll also serve him right for hitting on her behind his brother's back! Jayden will go seriously mental.

So now all I have to do is keep myself occupied until the

balance of the universe is restored. I hear my mum come in the door and make the usual greetings.

"Here, Harry. Here, Harry," she calls. "Look at you! Good dog."

It's like she looks forward to seeing that mutt more than she does me. I decide to make one more attempt on the mobile front. It's been almost a week now and being without it is killing me. Didn't I say that a sharp, fatal blow to the head from my mother would be a better way to die? I was so right.

I walk to the kitchen and see my mother whacking a frozen lasagna into the oven and then pouring herself a massive glass of red wine.

"Get off there, Camilla! Get off NOW!" she screeches at the cat.

I make a tactical decision not to ask her about getting a new phone.

"Hi darling," she says wearily. "Can you watch this lasagna and get it ready for dinner? I've spent the afternoon in Diana's Bouquet and I have a massive headache. I hate jonquils. They stink! I'm going to have a bath."

When I see her drag herself towards the bathroom and leave her phone on the counter, I pounce and ring Will. He'll be back from surf camp now, surely.

"Yeah," Will drawls.

Again, the sound of his voice washes the doubts away. I'm so excited to talk to him. It's been four whole days! I've been having major Will withdrawal pains. I ask him what surf camp was like. Did he catch any good waves? Did Mr. Battenburg, the Year Ten coordinator, get any? Or was he a total wipeout like last year? Who did Will hang out with? What was the food like? Any embarrassing gossip?

I ask him all this, even though the only thing I really want to know is, *did you miss me?*

"It was all, you know, cool," says Will.

And that's it for the whole surf camp topic. Sigh! He really isn't into talking on the phone. Then I ask him what he's doing tonight?

"Nothing much," he yawns. "Weather's pretty bad. I might stay in."

I tell him I can come over to his, or he can come to mine and we can maybe watch a DVD or ... something. (I'm thinking smooching in The Dungeon.)

"Nah, I can't. Mum's making us all a big dinner – some Spanish rice thingo. What ...?" (And here Will calls to his mother, who must be standing close by.) "Paella ... Mum says it's called paella. Anyway, she wants me to stay in so ..."

So there goes my Friday night! I tell him I *really* need to see him this weekend and he mumbles back that if the surf's good he might go to Hammerhead tomorrow. I ask him what time, exactly, he'll be there ('cos we can't ring each other).

"Uh, look, I'm not sure –" He hesitates. "Gotta see what the surf's doing. I can't make it blow offshore whenever I want. I can't tell you what I've done and where I'm gonna be every minute of every day. I'll see you, so stop stressing out on me."

I'm so surprised by his tone of voice that I ring off and dump the phone on the counter. It's like a chill winter wind has stirred the branches of Lothlórien wood.

This is Jai's scabby work! I'll bet Will has seen the pics and, just as Jai wanted, every time Will thinks of me he sees me covered in yogurt, dribble or hair. This is beyond depressing! After all, aren't I Will's "little leg rope"? He always says that I'm strong and independent and he's never complained before that I crowd him. Maybe I am giving him a hard time. Without my mobile I can't help thinking that everyone's talking behind my back.

I didn't get to mention the dance coming up soon. There's lots of stuff to arrange. Who's dropping us off? Who's picking us up? What are we going to *wear*? I have to look OTT this year and with money tight *and everything* I'll probably be forced to make a secret raid on the heap of clothes on Tilly's floor. I know she's got some great stuff – somewhere under there. Even if Will is a bit turned off by those pics of me, my utterly gorgeous Tilly ensemble will obliterate them from his mind!

I drag my sorry self back to The Dungeon and slump in my chair. When I look at the screen I see that there's an eye2eye from Bianca on FacePlace.

Hey Els. Reeelly miss U. Jai out with boys. Wanna catch movie? BXXX

In truth, about the last person on earth I want to see is Bianca Ponsford, but then I remember what Dad says: "Keep your friends close, and your enemies closer."

I Google this saying and find out it's by Sun Tzu, who wrote this book called *The Art of War* in 400 BC or something like that. It's all about the strategies you should use against your enemy when you are going into battle. This dude's also got a couple of other ideas that appeal:

- *O divine art of subtlety and secrecy! Through you we learn to be invisible, through you inaudible; and hence we can hold the enemy's fate in our hands.*
- *All warfare is based on deception.*
- *Hence, when able to attack, we must seem unable; when using our forces, we must seem inactive; when we are near, we must make the enemy believe we are far away; when far away, we must make him believe we are near.*

With all this in mind I write back to Bianca:

C U at Majestic in 1 hour.
EXXX

I have to keep Bianca close to me so that she doesn't try to meet Jai and ruin Tilly's little surprise party. I have to make it seem like I'm totally, randomly in the moment with her as a BF even though I am plotting her boyfriend's downfall. I hate to deceive Bianca, but this is the ancient, divine art of warfare and she has, unfortunately, aligned herself with my enemy. She is a part of the Axis of Evil. Her fate is now in my hands!

I am just about to get dressed when there's a *ping* on the computer and I see it's an eye2eye from Carmelita:

> *Hey Elly.*
>
> *I've been checking out Jai's FacePlace and some of the pages of the crew at Oldcastle High and there are heaps of people paying out on him!*
>
> *I reckon you are totally winning the war on Jai. He's a bully and a jerk! You look funny and cute and adorable in those pics.*
>
> *Sometimes people get jealous of you (and only a Total BFF can tell you that). But those pics just make them see how fun you are! And why I miss you soooo much!!!*
>
> *So stay strong and don't mind what others say. Everything will be cool. Luv ya! Miss ya heaps!*
>
> *Carmelita XXX*

Erk! Could this be true? When I go to Jai's FacePlace and brave the vile pics one more time, I see that there are in fact a lot of messages paying out on him.

> UR stupid, Jai.

> Wot a lowlife!

Not fair. UR nasty and mean.

Got pix of Jai in his undies – anyone wanna see?
  Eeeyew! No tks.

Elly's got more class in her little finger than Jai's got in his whole body.

Honestly, I feel like crying. Goes to show there is some justice in cyberspace after all! When I think of Tilly's plan, I wonder if we might be going too far. I remember that I felt a bit uneasy about it when she first told me. I hear Tilly's door slam in the South Wing and I tear into the kitchen. She's grabbing her car keys off the hook and winding a leopard-print chiffon scarf around her slim neck.

"*It's payback time!*" she sings.

I babble that I'm not sure that we should do it. Maybe Sun Tzu's got the whole thing wrong and ... Well, surely the ultimate "Art of War" is to avoid war?

"*What* are you talking about?" demands Tilly.

I realize I sound like a nutter, but I tell her that maybe Jai and Bianca didn't mean it and that –

"Don't be a total doormat," snaps Tilly. "You have to show Jai you can't be stomped on. You have to stand up to bullies. And the idea that a Year Nine boy can think he's got a chance with a Year Twelve girl? *Forget* about it! On that score alone, he has to be crushed like an ant."

Crushed like an ant? Hmmm, that sounds pretty good.

"As for Bianca? Maybe if she gets rid of Jai, she can get a nicer boy. We'll be doing her a favor." And then, with a swish of chiffon and a stolen waft of Mum's Coco perfume, Tilly's off out the door.

Half an hour later, I am too. And it's only when the bus stops outside the Majestic Movieplex that I remember the lasagna in the oven.

Friday night.
Six days PM.

Bianca makes the weird choice to see *He's Just Not That Into You*, starring Jennifer Aniston (Best Hair Ever Award for years running), Scarlett Johansson, Drew Barrymore and Jennifer Connelly. In fact, in the hair department it's a total five-star fest.

The thing that's depressing, though, is that in every relationship in the movie, one person is into it more than the other one. Could that be me and Will? I shake off this idea. Will and I have been going out together for ten months and I know by now that there's only one thing he is into more than me — a six-foot offshore cyclone swell. No girlfriend of a surfer could ever compete with that. It's hard to take, but it's a fact.

Bianca's bawling into her second purse pack of tissues and honking like a llama when the lights come up. I steer her towards Cromwell Café. The walk might give her a chance to pull herself together.

I'm surprised that it actually feels good to be out walking in the main street of Oldcastle with Bianca tonight. It's cold and we pull our hoodies over our heads (even though it crushes our hair) and mash our hands into our pockets.

We both look fab – me in a gray wool minidress cinched with a red leather belt, thick black tights and black suede ankle boots. Bianca's wearing kitten heels, jeans, a gorgeous glittery black long-sleeved top and this totally great blue fake-fur shrug tied with a satin ribbon. Pity we have to wear our hoodies over the top. But it's not like anyone's going to care much in the streets of Oldcastle on a freezing Friday night.

We stop and look in the window of Princess Slippers and I spot a divine pair of purple wedge shoes that look like they're made out of some sort of sleek plastic. Bianca gives them the nod. She's texting like crazy, as per usual, but in those rare intervals when she gives me her full attention, we are totally connecting.

There are a few people out and about – the usual crowd hanging in front of the London Tavern, puffing on cigarettes and shivering in the night air. Then, even with her hoodie pulled almost over her eyes, Bianca spots a full-on fashion disaster.

"Don't look, Elly," she gasps. "White stretch denim jeans, silver sequin tank top and pink flip-flops getting out of a taxi. I said, DON'T LOOK!"

I manage not to swivel my head the whole way and I'm proud of myself. Months of training from Bianca have finally paid off. When we walk past and I see the actual crime, I high-five Bianca – it's definitely an eleven on the drack-o-meter and well spotted.

Soon we are sitting in Cromwell's, sipping on hot chocolate and hogging a basket of chips smothered in salt and ketchup and, really, despite everything that's happened, it's just like old times.

"I want to tell you something, El," says Bianca, looking up at me with her wide blue eyes as she tries to prod her squashed do into place. Her hair looks like a punched-in profiterole. "I am soooo sorry for what Jai did with the photos."

It looks like she's going to cry again.

"You were right. Jai found them when he borrowed my phone. I had a massive fight with him tonight and I finally made him take them off FacePlace," Bianca sniffs. "I told him I would break up with him if he didn't."

Ulp! This so isn't what I was expecting and I stuff hot chips in my mouth so I don't have to reply. OW! I burn my tongue but try not to let it show.

"The thing is – " Bianca wipes ketchup off her cheek and continues – "Jai has this stupid sense of humor sometimes, and he told me he thought the photos would be funny."

As if! I heard Jai on the radio saying I hated his guts. "Bad pictures of Elly" – that's what he said. I take a mouthful of water to soothe my scorched mouth and, again, just nod as Bianca goes on.

"I thought you'd think they were funny too. I see now I got that wrong. Part of him wanted to get back at Will after they had that fight. You know that the football heads and the surfie boys have this full-on war going at school. But they should leave us girls out of it. I told him our friendship means a lot to me. And it does ... truly."

She's saying all this really seriously and tearing her napkin into little pieces with her black fingernails.

"Hey, you can get a pizza anytime! Right? But best friends are hard to find. So the pics are gone now and ... I'm sorry. I never wanted us to be enemies ... Even if you did lose that photo of me with Hugh Jackman."

Bianca reaches a hand across the table and I squeeze it. I'm guilty of a criminal act. As I've already admitted, losing that photo is unforgivable.

What would Sun Tzu do right now? I'm sort of *subtle*, *secretive* and *inaudible*, but only because I can't think of anything to say. When I think of what Tilly has in store for Jai tonight, I feel sick.

"I love Jai so much," says Bianca, as she stirs a melting pink marshmallow into her hot chocolate. "He really is kind underneath. You should see the cards he writes me! He tells me how much he loves me every minute of every day."

I stare down into the basket of chips, noticing every tiny grain of salt. Will has never told me he loves me. He's never written a card to me. I can't believe it. I'm jealous of Bianca and Jai! But then I remember that Tilly says Georgie Daniels told her Jai's always trying to sleaze onto Lily Cameron. It would break Bianca's heart if she knew what a gutter rat he was. I decide to keep this fact to myself.

"I know that Jai and Will don't like each other," says Bianca, honking again into a teensy scrap of napkin. "But they're both so different. If we really try, maybe they'll be friends one day. I'd hate to think they ever came between us."

I give Bianca's hand another squeeze and tell her that I feel the same. And right at this moment I really believe what I am saying. We should try to make peace between our boyfriends. We're like Hillary and Condoleezza in the Middle East. Bianca smiles gratefully and looks up at me like an innocent guinea pig, not knowing that Tilly's about to drop a brick on her furry blonde head.

And then Bianca's phone rings and it's Jai. He's at the football game! At least, I hope he is. If I had a phone right now I'd tell Tilly to call this whole thing off.

Bianca laughs and giggles. Jai's telling her the football score – Sovereigns 20, Regents 10 – so he really is at the game. Phew!

I'm watching a red rash creep up Bianca's neck and her eyes shining with happiness. She really is in love with that idiot. What can you say? Bianca pushes the plate of chips closer to me and I'm reminded of what Grandpa Pickering always reckons: *Every Jack has his Jill*.

Friday night, again.
Six days PM.

By the time I get back to The Dungeon it's almost midnight. I immediately check Jai's FacePlace and the pics have vanished! Gone to the great big Trash File in the sky. All the comments – the good and the bad – have been erased as well.

I have my life back. Yahoo!

I crash out, happy that this vile chapter of my existence is closed. At last!

Saturday morning.
One week PM.

I wake up at 6:30 to a ding on my computer and an eye2eye from Carmelita. It's unbelievably early, but then again she's probably been awake since dawn feeding Viscount the pig and ... er ... tending the nuts (or whatever it is you have to do with macadamias).

> *El.*
> *This is the WORST, ever. You have to call me. Beg, borrow or steal a phone! I'm here for ya (even in Queensland). Remember that.*
> *Love ya!!!!*
> *Carmelita XXX*

Huh? What's she talking about? It's not like Carmelita to think the worst about anything. My stomach does a hideous back flip and I can feel every single hair on my head vibrating with electricity.

I pull on my dressing gown and creep down the hall to the South Wing – like a downstairs maid in the halls of Buckingham Palace trying not to wake the slumbering Royal Family. I open Tilly's bedroom door a crack and see the corner of her mobile peeping out from under her pillow. Her room is the usual smelly trash heap and getting to the phone is not going to be easy. As my eyes adjust to the gloom, I see a few stepping stones of beige carpet and I pick my way through the obstacle course.

My fingers touch the corner of the phone and I carefully extract it from under Tilly's nest of dark brown hair. She stirs and snuffles, but doesn't wake up. I carefully edge back through the pile with the precious phone in my hand and step on a massive buckled handbag. Mercifully there's no "crunch" of plastic sticks of lip balm and I leap for the door in a mighty bound. Even before I'm back in The Dungeon, I'm dialing Carmelita's number.

"Hey, Elly!" Carmelita's voice is unnaturally cheery for this early. "How are you, babe?"

I know she has bad news and I politely ask her to get on with it.

"It's Will."

What about Will? I want her to spill her guts right this

instant.

"Well, this morning I was up early cleaning out Viscount's pen and when I came back in there was a message from Lily Cameron's FacePlace."

Lily Cameron? Carmelita hardly knows her. What sort of weird coincidence is this? My nerves are at critical load and I'm about to black out with the suspense.

"Well, if you go to Lily's mirror, there are, er ... pictures there of her in the spa with, um ... oh, Elly, it's *Will*."

I'm not sure I actually say anything at this point. I look out the window just to make sure that I'm still on Planet Earth. For one stupid moment I focus on the last shriveled apricot on our tree.

"I hate being the one to tell you, Elly," moans Carmelita. "But I thought you'd better know now."

With Tilly's mobile clamped to one sweaty ear, I log on to Lily's site. I'm one of her 194 friends. Oldcastle High's not a big school so pretty much everyone is "friends" with everyone else – whether they particularly want to be or not. No one dares *not* be friends.

And OH. OH. OH! I drop the phone on my desk and both hands are over my mouth and I'm silently screaming. It's like someone's taken to Lothlórien woods with a chainsaw. Aaaaargh! Aaaaargh!

It *is* Will. Even though the images are dark and a bit blurry, I'd know that mop of blond curls anywhere. He's in a spa. He's got his head thrown back and he's laughing. There are Lily Cameron's ten red toenails. She's sitting opposite him, her feet propped up on his tanned chest. She's smiling like a fox about to pounce on a marsupial.

And that's not the only picture. In the next one, Lily's sitting alongside Will and he's got his arm around her shoulder – she's under the golden branch that should be sheltering me! At least she's got a bathing suit on. Although there's nothing to be grateful for when I see that Will is smiling and looking at *her* with the same big brown eyes that should be looking at *me*.

There's one more burnt stick to poke in my eyes. In the third picture Will is standing by the edge of the spa and holding Lily's hand as she climbs out of the swirling water. His other hand is on her hip. They're gazing at each other with … what is it? I don't want to give that look a name or I'll vomit.

And then someone must have called "cut" on the scene because that's all there is. I scroll and click like a maniac. Then what happens? Where do they go after this? And after that? But there are no more pics and it's like I have just seen the trailer to the most terrifying horror movie of all time.

I spot the post from Lily:

Oooh, look who '"dropped in" last night. Mr. Will "six foot plus and perfect" Phillips. Both of us makin' waves at my place ☺

I should be crying by now. Maybe I am. I don't know,

91

because it's like my brain has stopped sending messages to my body. The telephone pole's fallen over. The satellite has crashed from the sky. The cable is melted. The line is dead.

Somehow a flicker of information gets through and I reach for the mobile.

"Els ... Elly? Are you still there?" Carmelita is frantically calling.

I must make some sort of noise because she hears I am still here. Wherever "here" is.

"Oh, I just don't know what to say," she groans. "Maybe it isn't as bad as it looks, maybe ..."

Her voice trails off because she knows that it's totally *worse* than it looks. There's nothing under the burning sun or the pale moon, in the wind or the swirling tides that can make this better than it looks.

"If that's what Will's really like," Carmelita says, "then you're better off without him."

And it's the words "without him" that finally make me hang up and cry out loud. I'm hardly even able to walk as I feel my way down the hall to Tilly's room. I lean against the door frame, snap on the light and then just stand there, paralyzed.

Tilly sits up rubbing her eyes and turns to me. I manage to get out a messy sentence that I think includes the words "Will," "Lily" and "FacePlace." Tilly looks at me, her perfect, pretty mouth turns down and she falls back on her pillow, shielding her face from the light with one thin white arm.

"What? Oh, no, Eleanor. I was hoping you wouldn't find out. Not on the Net anyway."

I stumble through the piles of Tilly's clothes and fall on my knees by her bed. I bury my face in her T-shirt and sob into her stomach. Tilly reaches out and strokes my hair as she speaks.

"It all went horribly wrong, Els. We were all there – me, Lily and Georgie Daniels – and it was just like we planned. We fired up the spa and then we rang Jai. He said he was at the game with Jayden and couldn't come. We rang three times, we texted, and he still wouldn't come. I was in the family room. I was going to put on a DVD and forget about the whole stupid idea, when I heard Will's voice at the front door."

I wipe my eyes on Tilly's shirt and then sit back. I want to hear this. Every. Hideous. Detail.

"I waited until I could corner Lily and I asked her, 'What's Will doing here?' She just laughed and said, 'Who knows?' But I have to tell you, Els, I think she was expecting him to come over. Maybe she was hoping Jai would be there too and they'd – I dunno, have a fight or something."

A million questions are running around in my head. But I don't know where to start, so I let Tilly go on.

"I couldn't think what to do. Should I go out there so Will would see me and go home? Or should I just let the whole thing unfold. This wasn't 'entrapment,' Els. I promise. This was more about catching someone committing a crime of their own making."

My body is shaking, but I'm saying "uh-huh" at the same time, not wanting Matilda to leave anything out.

"I decided to leave and I told Georgie that if anything happened, to make sure she got the evidence on her mobile. So I could show you. You're my sister. I'd want you to know."

I nod again. Go on.

"And now the photos are on the *Net*? Georgie and Lily must have done it after Will left."

I can't seem to get any air into my lungs through the tears and snot. I wipe my nose on Tilly's quilt.

"I kept thinking about Lily and wondering why I trusted her in the first place. It's not like she's one of my best friends. Maybe I was just blinded by wanting to get revenge on Jai. But I don't get it – why would Lily and Georgie do that?"

It's exactly what that site said: *Emotions and the Internet don't mix.* Well, too late, they're mixed up now.

"I'm going to murder Georgie when I see her." Tilly sits up and punches her pillow. "I can't believe she'd do something so disgusting! And why would Lily want Jayden to see the photos anyway? It just doesn't make sense."

I've heard enough now. I try to get to my feet to walk away, but it's easier to crawl. So that's what I do – I crawl through Tilly's underwear and jeans and tops and shoes. Tilly scrambles out of bed and tries to drag me to my feet, but I don't want to stand. Leave me down here with the lowly things that squirm and slither in the shadows.

☹☹☹☹

Saturday morning.
Later. One week PM.

I can't say how long it took for the tears to slow. But there was a point when I looked out the window of The Dungeon and saw that the heavy gray clouds hanging over Oldcastle were being blown out to sea by an offshore wind. That's when I knew I'd find Will on Winchester Headland. He's spent hours patiently teaching me how to watch the weather so I know when big surf is running. He might come to regret that.

I'm scrambling up the old stone stairs, two at a time, and the wind is twisting my hair into ropes that slap my face. When I get to the top and see him, what will I say? What will I do?

I want to push him onto the rocks below and watch the

surf suck him under then throw him up again, bashing him senseless into the cliff face.

And then I see him in that familiar pose, shading his eyes. Looking for a wave. My heart breaks and snaps like a fiberglass surfboard – tumbled and tossed and swept out to sea in fragments that can never be reassembled.

He turns and spots me. In that moment, in his surprise and confusion, I see that it's all true.

"Elly, what are you doing here? It's early. You're hardly dressed, you must be freezing," says Will.

I register that I'm still in the raggy old Britney Spears T-shirt and black pajama shorts I wear to bed. My bare feet are smeared with mud. I stop barely two feet from Will and ask him where he was last night.

"Elly ..." he begins, and he's half-smiling. I can't believe it.

He turns his head away so I can't look into his eyes. Those eyes that have always been such a soft gray, but this morning seem to reflect the black rocks in the cliff. He scuffs at the earth with his bare, tanned feet.

"It's like I told you, I stayed home, 'cos Mum was cooking ..." he mumbles.

I want to shout at him that he's a liar and a fake. That he cares more about a dead crab or a floating plastic bag than he does about me!

Instead I turn and run as fast as I can, fancying that I am Arwen Evenstar fleeing Lothlórien and my dearest love, forever.

"Elly, Elly!" Will calls.

I'm stumbling down the stone stairs, grabbing the railing to keep from falling. But I fall anyway, into a deep black hole of misery.

Saturday afternoon. One week PM. Three hours AW (after Will).

Where do I begin with the disaster that is my life? There are stacks of comments on Lily Cameron's FacePlace mirror already. Seems like the whole world has seen the pictures of Will and her. I can't resist going back again and again to look, like I'm witnessing some international crisis unfolding on CNN.

Oooh. Trouble in paradise!!!

Where there's a Will, there's a willing. LOL!

Where's Elly? Under the bubbles breathing through a straw?

Oops, Elly, he's just *not* that into you!

Silly Willy jumping at Lily's pad. Ribbit!

Jayden's gonna freak. Shld be worth watching.Heh.

C'mon guys. *Three pics?* That's all we get????

Ah, Will.It shoulda been me!:-)

Will and Lily
Sittin in a bath
When poor Elly sees them.
Boy, she's gonna barf!
Heh!
The Phantom Rhymer.

That jerk's right, I do feel sick. I turn off the monitor and creep to my bed. So this is what it feels like to have a broken heart. I know it sounds like a stupid thing to say, but I didn't think it would hurt this much.

Untold millions of wretched, sad people have written songs and stories and poetry about lost love. I've heard and read lots of them. But until now it was like they were talking about something I couldn't understand – like someone telling you what it feels like to walk on the moon.

I might as well have left the earth's orbit. I feel weird

and weightless. Even though I'm lying on my bed, it's as if I'm floating somewhere above a planet called Will and Elly, looking back on it through a black hole in space. The thought that I will never walk there again makes me cry until my ribs ache.

I haven't reached for the tissues because I want to feel every tear as it runs down my face, into my neck, and soaks the pillow. I want to remember every single salty drop. My eyelids are swollen and my fingers are puffy from clutching at the blankets. If I can just hold on here I might stop myself from spinning out past the stars into eternal blackness.

In a far-off somewhere I can hear a knock on my door and a *ping* on my computer. But don't they know I'm not here? I've gone. I'm drifting in an infinite cloud of sorrow …

Saturday night. One week PM. Eight hours AW.

I woke up in the early evening to find I'd slept for five hours. For about two seconds there I felt fine, but then reality hit me like a meteor strike.

I'm not with Will anymore.

:'-(CLAB

Now I'm on my computer and I Google "broken heart" and get 37,200,000 results. So there are more than 37 million of us who want to curl up and die? More than the entire population of Australia? It should make me feel better that I'm not alone. Instead it makes me feel stupid and ordinary.

There's a knock on the door of my dungeon and Mum's head appears. She's brought me a plate of leftover, slightly charred lasagna.

"Oh, honey, I heard what happened. Are you OK?" says Mum, making the right sort of sympathetic face.

If she really understood how I felt she'd be booking me a passage on a slow steamer to India with my spinster great-aunt. Isn't that how they mended broken hearts in the olden days? Just sent you away until you stopped wanting to throw yourself under a horse and carriage?

Instead she stands behind my chair and pats my head until I feel like Harry the dog.

"'The First Cut is the Deepest' – that's the name of a Cat Stevens song," Mum sighs. "Your Auntie Marg used to flog that song to death when she first had her heart broken, then she passed it on to me when I got dumped. It means that the first time your heart is broken is the worst."

Cat *who*? I'm sure this is supposed to make me feel better, but I'm not sure how. She can't seriously be thinking that I'll be up for having this happen to me *again*. I'll be off working in the slums in India before I give my heart to any boy again.

I don't say anything to Mum, but she won't take the hint and doesn't look like leaving. She's plonked herself on my bed and is cradling my pink stuffed pig. She wants to tell me all the minute historical details of her first broken heart. But, as she so often reminds me, she lived and loved in the Days Before the Internet Was Invented. She's got no idea – at all. She didn't have to endure the whole world having a grandstand view of her heart being smashed to smithereens.

I hand her back her burnt offerings, tell her I'm not hungry, I'm fine and I need to be by myself.

"Well, darling, I'm here if you need me and want to talk …" Mum says, for the millionth time since I was nine.

I tell her I know that by now, and thankfully she leaves.

On my computer there are three eye2eyes from Carmelita and two from Bianca. They'll want to talk, rehash, gossip and blame. And I'm just not ready yet. I trash all of them. Maybe it was better in the old days when people had to write letters and they took three days to reach you. At least by then you could open the envelope and read the letter without the print turning into an inky pond in front of your eyes.

Then it's Dad's turn to make an effort. I can see that he's squirming as he tiptoes in and perches on the wooden toy chest at the end of my bed. I must admit I feel sorry for him sometimes – it can't be easy to be a man surrounded by emotional females.

Although surely he's had enough practice with Tilly's broken hearts. She's had at least three bust-ups I can remember and we all had to creep around the house and not look at her for weeks on end. Tilly takes rejection really hard. And as bad as I feel right now, I'm determined not to be so pathetic.

"It's a tough business, all this 'love' stuff isn't it, *ma belle*?" says Dad.

And then I'm blubbering like a baby in his strong arms and being totally pathetic!

"Tilly showed Mum and me all that stuff there on the computer and, well ... I don't think Will can talk his way out of it, really. And what about all those nasty comments from the peanut gallery who want to put in their two cents' worth? Bet they wouldn't be so game if they had to put their names on there."

Again, if this is supposed to be cheering me up, it's a poor effort. Before I can stop him, Dad's off again.

"When I was a young bloke you could two-time girls all over town and never get caught. But now, when everyone's got a phone with a camera and computers to send photos, everyone has to be on their best behavior all the time!"

I'm now hiding behind a cushion out of sheer embarrassment. I don't want to hear about his love life either. Has he got something to hide?

"Not that I've ever done anything like that!" he says quickly. "I'm just thinking, that's all. I don't envy you having the Internet when you're trying to have a social life. There's too much information these days, if you ask me."

I hadn't asked him, actually. And surely Dad's not feeling sorry for Will?

"That boy's been a rat bag and a nuisance. In fact, he came over here to see you and I sent him packing quick-smart. I reckon I should build a moat around this house and put sharks in it."

Will came here? What did he want? What did he say? I know I shouldn't ask, but it's hard not to.

"I dunno what he wanted. I just told him to clear off. Good riddance! There'll be plenty of boys wanting to take you out, *ma belle*. Just you wait and see."

Groan! The old "plenty more fish in the sea" line. I was wondering how long it would be before someone came up with that one. Dad's finished his speech and he leaves.

Two down, one to go. Sure enough, there's a tap at my door and it's Tilly.

"I've found out what happened last night," she huffs, and sits on my bed.

I watch as she swishes her hair, pulls two of Nan's old clip-on daisy earrings off her ears and rubs at her flattened lobes. So she knows what happened. So what? Nothing will change unless she can tell me that Will has a secret twin brother … and one tiny fragment of my heart leaps with the possibility! Then my poor, tired brain kicks in and reminds me that I'm not starring in *The Bold and the Beautiful*.

"I caught up with Georgie and Lily and they told me the whole saga," sighs Tilly. "And it's so dumb, you wouldn't believe."

Try me. Could anything be as dumb as me thinking that Will loved me? Truly. I'm in the Guinness World Records for dumb. I nod to Tilly that she should go on as she flops back and traces her lips with a stick of beeswax.

"Jayden dumped Lily on Thursday and she didn't tell anyone. Not a soul."

This is odd. There's actually someone in Oldcastle who

doesn't blab continually about their entire life? Usually word of this stuff is out within hours ... or minutes. This was three days ago now.

"Obviously, if I'd known I would never have included her in the plan," Tilly says. "You can't trust the brokenhearted, Els. They're not really rational."

Hah! I know that. Right now I have this weird urge to wade through the fountain in Victoria Square and jump off the statue of King George in a silverbeet bikini!

"Her whole motivation was to get back at Jayden, and because I'd already suggested we get Jai into the spa, it played right into her hands. Of course we rang Jai and asked him to bring over pizzas, like I said, but he wouldn't come – and then Will turned up ..." Tilly hesitates and stops.

The question is, of course, why did Will go to see Lily when he was supposed to be seeing me?

"This is garbage, Els, but your so-called Prince Charming, that weasel, has been calling and texting Lily for the past week nonstop. She didn't take any of his messages 'cos she knew you two are ... were ... like, an item."

I shudder when she calls Will a "weasel." When I opened my eyes this morning he was still "wonderful Will." So he was calling and texting Lily even when he was away at surf camp? Will? The "free spirit" who's "not good on the phone"? I find this hard to believe.

"I know it's hard to believe," Tilly continues. "What happened was that Jayden found some of Will's texts, and even though Lily said she hadn't answered them, he went mental and dropped her on the spot. Then, the next night when Jai didn't turn up, she was thrilled when Will dropped by instead."

I wonder if he ate his mum's paella first?

"So this whole thing was to get back at Jayden. It wasn't about you at all."

Oh, OK then, nothing to do with me. My heart's just been bashed senseless by some random accident. That makes me feel better – not!

Tilly's guessed what I'm thinking and continues. "But I know that's no consolation, Els. I just want to say that you have to see that Will's the one who's wrong. He busted up Jayden and Lily and betrayed you. And to think that surfie flake gets around with this 'peace and love' act ..."

I finish the sentence in my head: *And to think that an idiot like me believed it.*

"No one saw this coming, Els, no one. So you can't blame yourself."

Too late.

"Georgie says her phone was out of batteries, so she just took some pics on Lily's phone – I'm not sure whether Will knew they were being taken or not. Then Georgie left and after that, Lily's poisoned mind got to work."

Another *ding* on my computer and I see it's an eye2eye from Will's little sister Pookie. If she's found out, all the way down there in the wooden shack at Hammerhead, then everyone in town must know. The poor baby will be wondering what's happening. That's the other thing that's painful. I loved spending time with Pookie. She's only nine and she's like my little sister. The thought that I won't be hanging out with her ever again is truly sad.

"I just want you to know that I will never, ever speak to Georgie again," Tilly rants. "She's guilty as far as I'm concerned. Guilty of being heartless and thoughtless. She's a total moron. And as for Lily ... flirting with Year Nine and Ten boys? Where's her self-respect? She's just not right in the head. I wouldn't even have started talking to her if I hadn't bought this bracelet from her last summer."

Tilly holds her tiny wrist up to the desk lamp. The bracelet's a pretty thing with tiny, dangling pink glass beads and shells. Maybe that's why Will wants to be with her – 'cos she's clever and artistic and makes beautiful jewelry. Lily has big black shiny eyes like a possum, long dark hair, fair skin and laughs all the time. I can see her now with her red bathing suit and matching toenails. She knows how to do all that girly stuff boys love. The last time I matched my bathing suit and toenail polish was – never. Why is she always laughing? What's so funny, anyway? I catch my face in the mirror. I'm frowning, as usual.

I think too much, that's my problem. I ask too many questions.

"You know what you should do, Els?" says Tilly. "You should fight fire with fire."

Huh? Tilly's on her feet now, pacing my room, punching my pink pig repeatedly and looking quite scary, actually. What's she talking about? *Fire with fire.* Isn't this what got me into trouble in the first place?

"Well, OK, maybe not fire with fire, but how do you fight fire? With a big bucket of water! Here's the plan."

Another plan from Tilly? I slump forward over my desk with my head in my hands.

"What you do is put up a message on your FacePlace – how you're thrilled to be by yourself and that you've already moved on from Will. Then you post some photos of you looking gorgeous, independent and happy."

But, I moan, I'm not any of those things right now!

"Doesn't matter. This is all about perception, Els. You can't be a victim. Show everyone you're strong. That'll pour water on the flames of all this gossip once and for all. When I busted up I cried and carried on for ages. I was totally pathetic and useless and I look back on it now and think, if only I had been stronger! No one respects you for being weak."

But I do feel weak. Very weak. I'm starving hungry and I'm thinking about that burnt lasagna with affection. All the crying of the past few hours has zapped all the energy from my body. I feel floppy, like a Beanie Baby with a hole in it.

"I can help you if you like," says Tilly, with a glint in her eye.

I've seen that look before and it's dangerous. I tell Tilly I'll have a think about it. First she can help by bringing me something to eat. Before I expire. Please? Tilly agrees to bring supplies. She closes the door behind her.

The Dungeon is suitably gloomy tonight. Mum and Dad are down there in the family room watching TV. The wind and rain have started up again and the branches of the apricot tree are scraping at the window. It's exactly what you'd expect to find out the window of your "heartbreak hotel" if you were the loser character in a weepy movie.

I wonder what Will's doing? Is he sitting looking out the window and thinking of me too? Or up to his neck in bubbles with Lily? I've got an unread message from Pookie. I know it will make me cry. My fingers are just straying to the mouse when Tilly comes back with a bowl of microwaved lasagna (which has now been reheated twice and I half-hope lands me in intensive care with salmonella) and a packet of Tim Tams (she says they're essential heartbreak food).

Tilly watches me scoff everything with sisterly sympathy and after I've eaten I start to feel a bit more energized. Tilly looks over my shoulder at the computer screen and sees the eye2eye from Pookie. There's another *ding* that makes us both jump. It's from Will. *From Will!* Before my fingers can edge towards the mouse, Tilly pounces with a speed that would put Camilla to shame and hits "delete" – twice. The messages from Pookie and Will vanish. Just to make sure I can't get to them she empties the trash file as well.

"And that's the other thing," Tilly declares. "You will not speak to or see Will again. In fact, it's rule number one. No exceptions. Now have another Tim Tam and get to work."

111

Tilly exits, leaving behind a faint smell of blackberry hair conditioner and beeswax. I wonder whether I should take more advice from my big sister?

I've watched Tilly make her way in the world from when she first went to high school in her ugly blazer and clompy shoes with her hair in two sticky-out pigtails. I've seen all the tantrums and tears and bust-ups and arguments over the years. Now she's almost eighteen and look at her! Beautiful and smart and popular. She's deputy school captain. She's in the orchestra, on the swimming team and she won a state prize for chemistry. Total brainiac!

Everyone knows her boyfriend Eddie. He's a big hero here in Oldcastle – in the whole of Britannia, come to that. Tilly and Eddie were in the social pages of the *Britannia Bugle* last week at a charity night for the Prince John Hospital. Tilly looked like Princess Mary of Denmark and Eddie looked like Prince Frederick – only taller, darker and on steroids.

So I hear what Tilly says, but I can't help wondering what Sun Tzu would say about all this. I Google *The Art of War* again and come up with this:

- *The difficulty of tactical maneuvering consists in turning the devious into the direct, and misfortune into gain.*
- *On the field of battle the spoken word does not carry far enough: hence the institution of gongs and drums. Nor can ordinary objects be seen clearly*

enough: hence the institution of banners and flags.

· *Gongs and drums, banners and flags, are means whereby the ears and eyes of the host may be focused on one particular point.*

· *Let your rapidity be that of the wind, your compactness that of the forest.*

· *In raiding and plundering be like fire, in immovability like a mountain.*

· *Let your plans be dark and impenetrable as night, and when you move, fall like a thunderbolt.*

So, Tilly's right. I need to turn my misfortune around, and in a hurry. The gongs and drums? Well, as this Sun Tzu dude said back in 400 BC, the spoken word doesn't carry fast enough. As for the banners and flags? You can do all that on the Net. My words will be as fast as the wind and they will fall like thunderbolts.

:-(0) MAKE MY DAY

Saturday. Midnight. One week PM. Twelve hours AW.

My FacePlace site is locked and loaded! I'm looking at it one last time before I unleash its power.

Once I got started, it was like I couldn't stop. All the incriminating pics are there now – the stupid, cringe-worthy ones of Will laughing with ginger beer coming out of his nose; Will falling over a railing wrestling with his wetsuit; Will playing the ukulele with his feet; Will with two dead starfish on his eyes.

I put them all in a slideshow and then backed it with that song from Rihanna – the one where she says the boy is only sorry 'cos he got caught and he'd better take off before she turns on the lawn sprinklers. Yeah!

I used to think these shots were *adorable* – that they showed Will's funny side. But now I can see what everyone else does – that underneath his "cool" image, he's just an immature idiot. No wonder Jai thinks he's up himself.

The photos were just a few of the hundreds of snaps I had to choose from. In the ten months we were going together I took zillions of pics. I should erase them all I suppose, but it's not as satisfying as ripping up a real photo. There are a couple of pics of Will and me that I printed out and stuck on my corkboard. I'll get around to tearing them down later.

With Camilla winding herself around my ankles and settling down to sleep on my feet, I found a quote about "lost love":

> *It is best to love wisely, no doubt; but to love foolishly is better than not to be able to love at all.*
>
> William Makepeace Thackeray

I posted it and then I cried some more and Camilla looked up at me with two sweet round orange eyes like clementines. Just for her sake I stopped blubbering and got on with it. Like Tilly said, this is all about "perception," AKA a pack of lies, because if I hadn't been so foolish and fallen in love with Will, I wouldn't be feeling so wretched. William Thackeray's wrong; I reckon it's safer not to love anyone, at all.

So I also added this:

The stupidest mistake in life is thinking the one who hurt you the most, won't hurt you again.

Anonymous

And that's *totally* true!

BTW, it's interesting that this quote's anonymous. Even way back then people wrote stuff anonymously, so it's not just the Net, Dad!

Then I got to work using my graphic design skills and made an animation – a hairy rodent with Will's head superimposed on it dancing across the page, wearing a T-shirt reading "Love Rat." It was a demented masterpiece.

Last, I posted some shots of me by myself – all the best ones I could find. Me looking, as Tilly said, "happy and independent." I dunno about "gorgeous," but in the ones I chose I'm smiling and the sun is out and yeah, I look like I don't have a care in the world. Maybe Will's right and everything in cyberspace is fake. Only I'm sure there was nothing fake in the photos of Will with Lily. It was all hideously authentic. And the pain I'm feeling is really, utterly real.

Now I see the page is ready and I send out an emergency bulletin informing my 105 friends (including the Prime Minister) that they should drop by my FacePlace and stare into the Mirror of Revenge!

Sunday. 2 a.m.
PM. AW.

I wake up to see the two crystal eyes of my pink pig staring at me accusingly, glittering in the moonlight. I *have* done the right thing trashing Will on the Net, haven't I? Tilly's right, isn't she? Surely Sun Tzu knew what he was talking about?

It's pitch black in The Dungeon and doubt strikes me like a thunderbolt.

Sunday. 10:30 a.m. PM. AW.

My computer *dinging* like crazy is the first sound I hear as I rub the sleep from my eyes. I see that already there are 13 new messages on my mirror. They seem to be mostly anonymous. (I left my mirror on lowest security so anyone could drop in and look. I reflect, in the cold light of morning, that maybe that wasn't the smartest thing to do.)

You go girlfriend!

This is a lesson for all boyz who cheat!

So Will's single? Xcellent.

Gotcha Will! Dumb seaweed head!

ROFL. Does this get any better?

Elly, I'd ask you out but now I'm scared! LOL

Say "cheese," Will, you RAT!!!

Jayden's revenge :-)

Can't wait till Monday morning.

Oooh Elly, you are a b****!

The Prime Minister is away from this site and will return on
October 19.
(Auto reply)

I miss you heaps. I hope you and Will get back together,
Pookie XoXoXo

Now Elly's dumped on Willy,
She says it's payback time,
Willy's lookin foolish,
Elly's lookin fine.
The Phantom Rhymer

Oh, help! I feel like I've been whacked in the head again, repeatedly and really hard. Where do I start with all this? Looks like both me and Will have been flamed. I don't know what to feel. What was I expecting?

:+(

Then I hear my mum calling from the hall.

"Eleanor, come on sleepyhead! I want you to help me get this house sorted out before we go to Nan's. There's a load of washing for you to hang out, then you can vacuum the family room and do the vegetable crisper for me. It's like a wilderness area in the bottom of that fridge!"

I yell to Mum that I'll be there in a minute, stalling for time. She seems to have already forgotten that I am an emotional basket case and need extra care right now.

My hand is shaking as I go to my mailbox and see there are eye2eyes from both Carmelita and Bianca. I open the one from Carmelita first:

El,
I don't think this was a good idea. I know you're angry and upset, but shouldn't you go and work this out with Will in private? I've been thinking, something about this doesn't make sense. Have you actually asked Will what was going on in those pics?
Luv ya, Carmelita XOXOXO

"Come on, Elly!" Mum barges in the door and stands there with her hands on her hips. "I want this house done. I'm not spending all my precious weekend cleaning up after everyone!"

I mumble that I'm coming and open the eye2eye from Bianca:

Hah!
U really nailed Smelly Willy!! He dezerves everything Ur dishing out.
Jai v.v. happy and Jayden will punch his head in for U.
Bianca. ☺ ☺ ☺

"ELLY, GET YOURSELF IN HERE RIGHT THIS MINUTE!" Mum screeches.

I wonder what Sun Tzu and his armies in 400 BC China would have done if they were confronted by a fire-breathing dragon? Run away and jump into the Yangtze River is my guess. Right now hanging out the washing and cleaning out the vegetable crisper sounds like as good a thing to do as any other.

The thought that I've made Jai "v.v. happy" makes me feel like I'm going to throw up.

✳

I'm piling yellow broccoli, bendy carrots and disgusting brown lettuce onto the kitchen counter and thinking that this vegetable crisper is like my life. All that was good and healthy just days ago has turned into rotten, moldy mush.

Tilly walks into the kitchen in an old, fraying pink silk

121

kimono. She sees me, stretches her arms and smiles. She looks so innocent this morning. It's hard to believe that I'm up to my armpits in stinking compost because of her. Because, when I think about it, if she hadn't suggested I get back at Jai and then at Will on the Net, I'd still be snapping fresh and full of wholesome goodness. As it is, I'm like this sad zucchini. You can poke your finger in me and what's underneath the skin is a rancid, gooey mess.

I watch as Tilly swigs from a carton of coffee-flavored milk.

"So, how's the battle on the Internet going, Els? Have we finished off the enemy once and for all?"

I just shove the clean crisper back in the fridge and brush past her. A couple of mouse clicks and she'll find out soon enough. Just like the rest of the world.

"Eleanor? Hello? Did you do what I said, or what?" Her voice echoes down the hall after me.

I don't know what to say, or think. Why can't I just be like laughing Lily Cameron and string beads onto thread, make pretty bracelets and necklaces instead of having to wrestle with all these jumbled words and thoughts?

Sunday. 3 p.m.
PM. AW.

Another Sunday afternoon and a classic roast dinner with
Nan. I only picked at a few of the edges of the crunchy
potato (my fave bits). Thinking about everything that's
happened, my stomach was still doing tumble-turns.
Thankfully, Mum and Dad decided to lay off nagging me to
eat and went for a walk to St. James Park to burn off their
Yorkshire puddings.

I'm helping Nan with the washing up in her funny old
kitchen. The dark green paint on the cupboards is cracked
and peeling, the red paint on the wooden countertops is
faded and the walls are a soft old yellow. She's got a row of
plain white plastic pots with blooming pink geraniums on
the windowsill. I love this place, and as the spring sunshine

lights up the room, I think there's no place on earth I'd rather be.

As long as I can remember, Nan's kitchen has been exactly the same as it is this afternoon. There's the chair with the carved kookaburra on the back. There's the old biscuit tin with pictures of wattle on the lid. There's the wooden dresser where the teacups all dangle in a row from their little metal hooks. I feel like I'm still a baby girl when I'm at Nan's and today I think it would be good to go back to being small enough to sit on her knee.

It's not like Nan's *really* old – she's not quite seventy yet. Grandpa Pickering is eighty-two! But Nan is proud of being old-fashioned. She's lived in the same house here in Port Britannia since after she was married. It's where Mum and Auntie Marg were raised. Dad thinks she might like to get away from the noise of the coal-loading terminal and the hoot of the tugboats and go to a retirement village that has a pool and golf course. Nan says the silence would drive her mad! (And she's always hated golf.)

Her little house is perched at the top of the street and looks as if it might roll down the hill any moment. It's the same steep hill that Pop walked down to go to work on the docks for almost forty-five years. I wonder if Nan sometimes imagines that he might walk in the door one day, covered in coal dust and carrying a bag of prawns and oysters for supper.

It was Pop's lungs that gave out in the end. He would sit

for hours on the front veranda, smoking and watching the supertankers being loaded at the dock, but he barely had breath to walk to the gate. I used to bring in the mail from the mailbox. Sometimes there were letters from his cousins back in Manchester, England, and I used to sit on the step and read them to him.

Nan and I are standing at the sink. She doesn't have a dishwasher, so I'm using her Royal Golden Jubilee memorial dish towel to do the drying. She's had this dish towel for seven years. I don't know whether this means that Nan doesn't have that many dishes to dry, or that this is a very well made dish towel.

I'm slowly wiping a saucer with Queen Elizabeth II's nose when Nan pulls the plug on the soapy water and turns to me. The sun's shining through her silver perm and she looks like she's wearing a crown. Her name's Elizabeth too, after the Queen Mother. And that's funny, 'cos Nan's the mother of my mother who's named Elizabeth after our Queen! Her smiling face is on this dish towel that I'm now mashing into a bread and butter plate.

"I got a letter from the Queen at Buckingham Palace once," says Nan. "Would you like to see it?"

A letter from the Queen? The real Queen, herself? Nan's never mentioned this before.

I smooth out the dish towel and leave Her Majesty to dry on the front of the old gas stove. I follow Nan up the narrow hallway to her bedroom. I don't often go in Nan's bedroom.

The curtains are pulled shut and I can't see much, but I can smell mothballs and violet talcum powder. It's a fragrance I love, but it makes me sad 'cos it also reminds me that Pop's not here. If he was still with us I would also be able to smell the eucalyptus and Friar's Balsam that he used in the vaporizer on his bedside table.

MUSM

"Now, you're a lovely tall girl Eleanor, just like your sister Matilda," says Nan. "So be a dear and get the box down from the top of that shelf."

I stand on a little stool with spindly legs and pull down the box covered in floral paper.

"Let's bring it out to the dining table where we can have a good dig around in it," declares Nan. "Lots of treasures in there – if the moths haven't gotten to them."

Nan shifts a Wedgwood serving plate sitting on a little lace doily and places the box on the dining room table. She lifts the lid and I can see it's crammed full of bundles of yellowing envelopes tied with red ribbons. And there are roses! The smell of roses is really strong.

"Oh, isn't that wonderful!" exclaims Nan. "I can't believe I can still smell those divine red roses. That was the last bunch of flowers your pop gave me before he passed away. I dried them with a few tablespoons of orris root and popped them in here."

Nan lifts a dry stem from a silky bag and papery petals crumble and fall. I see her eyes begin to mist with tears and

I feel like crying myself. I lay my head on Nan's shoulder and she kisses my forehead. We are both remembering darling Poppy.

"Now," Nan sniffs and straightens her back, "where did I put that letter? It's got the royal seal on the back of the envelope."

But I don't want see that yet. I'm dying to see what's in these bundles of letters tied with ribbons.

"Oh, those?" smiles Nan. "They're love letters. From before your pop and I were married. He was away three years working on the Snowy Mountains Scheme as a laborer and wrote to me every week, without fail."

I've heard of the Snowy Mountains Scheme in Australian history class at school. It was where they diverted the melted snow from the rivers into massive dams and then through turbines to make hydroelectricity.

"Your pop's family sailed out to Australia from Manchester in England in 1955 and settled in Britannia. I suppose the name made them feel at home," Nan chuckles. "When your grandfather turned eighteen a year later, he got a job in the Snowy Mountains. We were already engaged to be married and all his savings went into putting a deposit on this cottage. It was an old place, even back then, but we did love it so. The same rose bush is still climbing around the front door to this day."

Nan and Pop were engaged when they were teenagers. Imagine if Tilly came home wearing an engagement ring.

Mum and Dad would freak!

I ask Nan if I can read one of Pop's letters and she picks out one bundle and carefully unties the ribbon. She opens an envelope and hands me the stiff, coarse sheet of paper inside. The words are written very neatly in lead pencil.

My dearest Bet Bet,

I hope this letter finds you well, my darling girl!

This morning I went fishing along one of the beautiful ferny mountain creeks. What a sight to see the rainbow trout jumping right out of the water, chasing swarms of dragonflies in the sun!

It is a strange thing to think that all around will be under the depths of the mighty Eucumbene Dam some time soon.

The old town of Adaminaby will be drowned, so they're moving more than a hundred buildings to a site five miles away to the northeast. They are even dismantling an old stone church to rebuild it in the new town. I met a man who had not long been married in that very church and he was most upset to see it so ruined.

It's sad and sorry work, Bet. Ten thousand people came here almost a century ago looking for gold and so much history will be lost. Many of the old-timers will be saying farewell to their family farms.

But I have to remind myself that it is all progress and when we are married we will turn on the electric lights in our home in Port Britannia and be jolly grateful to the army of people from all over the world who've come to work in the bush and build this New Country.

It's a gray Sunday afternoon and I've just seen a squirrel glider flash past the window of my hut. The scallywag had better find refuge soon. I can see the snow will be early this year!

Tonight the Italians are treating a few of the chaps to spageti and red wine. I am very much enjoying their food and company and perhaps I will teach you how to make spageti when I return home.

I miss you Bet and think of you always. You are never far from my heart my dearest love.

Your adoring fiancé,

Andy.

I stare at the words on the paper and can't quite believe that Pop wrote them more than half a century ago. Funny that he couldn't spell "spaghetti," but Nan says no one in Oldcastle had ever tasted spaghetti back then. And no one had ever heard of pizza either! Pop was just a bit older than Tilly when he wrote this letter and it's hard to imagine her traveling all the way across the world by ship and going to work in the bush. (Although I sometimes wish she would!

But where, oh where, would she plug in her flat iron?)

"Your pop had a rickety old wooden table in the hut he shared with three German boys," remembers Nan. "It was hard to get the paper and pencils and sometimes the snow made it impossible for the post to get through for weeks at a time – but he always wrote to me, every Sunday."

Looking closely at the paper I reckon I can see the grain of the wood table coming right through the lead pencil writing. As I look at this letter I can imagine Pop in the high country with the snow piled up against the window of his hut, far away from everything he knew and wondering what was happening in the outside world. I ask Nan how she could stand getting just one letter a week.

"Well, the world was so much bigger then, I suppose," Nan smiles. "We just didn't expect to hear from each other every day. I knew that I was always in his thoughts and he knew he was in mine, and that was enough for us. I spent hours daydreaming about your grandfather. It's not like you young people now who call and do those text things night and day. I suppose you're lucky to have one another on the end of the line – but the daydreaming was marvelous. Everything was bigger and brighter and better in my imagination."

Nan takes out a few more of the letters for me to read and they are all so beautiful I feel like crying again. Nan must have more than a hundred letters here in this box and in every one Pop tells her he loves her madly. I especially adore the ones that she sent back to Pop in the Snowy Mountains – written in lovely, loopy letters in ink on paper as fine as a butterfly wing. Pop saved every single one.

Then we find the letter from Buckingham Palace from when Nan was just eight years old. She embroidered a linen handkerchief with wattle and sent it to Princess Elizabeth (before she was crowned the Queen) as a wedding present. This letter is on stiff paper headed with a red coat of arms and written with a typewriter.

```
Miss Elizabeth Spencer
15 Tower Street,
Britannia,
New South Wales,
Australia


19th December 1947


Dear Elizabeth,
The Princess Elizabeth has asked me to
pass on her sincere appreciation for the
lovely present you sent on the recent
occasion of her marriage.
    The Princess is extremely fond of wattle
and your embroidery is certainly very fine.
    Your kind thought is much appreciated and
the Princess thanks you for your best wishes
```

for her and her husband Prince Phillip.

Yours sincerely,
Lady Meg Egerton
Lady-in-Waiting to Princess Elizabeth

"It was such a thrill to receive it," says Nan, smiling. "I remember taking that letter to read to the class at Britannia Public School. I was quite the celebrity there for a while and even got my picture in the *Britannia Bugle!* I have the clipping here somewhere ..."

Nan shuffles through the box, and eventually holds up a tattered scrap of brown newsprint. We are both disappointed to see that the silverfish have gnawed a hole right through her face and we can see clear through to the geranium pots in the kitchen.

"Well, that's that!" declares Nan. "I've been decapitated. I suppose that's one good thing about the technology now. I could have just Googled my name and the story would have been saved forever, and in full color. Do you know, I can even remember I was wearing a yellow ribbon in my hair the day that photographer from the *Bugle* came."

I am amazed. How does Nan know about Google?

"Well, dear, I do like to keep up with all that's going on in the world. It's not as if I'm in the middle of the Snowy Mountains in the 1950s. I've even been thinking about getting a personal computer. They have lessons at the library."

I look at Nan. Astonished.

"And if I did get online we could talk to each other all the time on FacePlace. I'd like that, I really would."

I tell Nan that I'd like it too. It would be great to have her online. I could ask Nan's advice, instead of consulting the Great Oracle Tilly or Sun Tzu – because what does some ancient Chinese warrior actually know about my life? I'm not sure that Nan wants to be walking through the battlefield that's FacePlace at the moment, although I could send her photos of the family (Mum's edited versions, anyway).

Nan carefully reties all the letters with ribbon.

"When I die, you can have these letters to pass on to your grandchildren, Eleanor. It will be a lovely way for you to remember me and hear my voice long after I'm gone."

I don't want to think of Nan dying and this dear little wooden cottage empty. But at least I will have this box of letters. It will be a precious bit of family history that I'll always treasure.

Then I realize that I don't have *any* letters – at all! Not one. And definitely not one from royalty! I've kept some old birthday cards and party invitations, but that's about it. All the texts and emails from Will and my friends have vanished and they might as well be sitting in the drowned post office at the bottom of Lake Eucumbene.

I'm reminded that I really should get around to putting all the thousands of photos on my computer onto a disk for safekeeping. Imagine if our house was flooded ... or burned in a bushfire? Just losing my phone was bad enough.

I read an old birthday card decorated with blue wrens that my Nan got on her twenty-first birthday from her mother. Here's my great-grandmother's greeting, right here in black ink!

Many happy returns for the day, dearest daughter. Your loving mother.

I shouldn't think it, but I wish I had some cards or love letters from Will to keep and tie with red ribbon! There might be an eye2eye I still have from him that I could print – but that's hardly romantic. I've got nothing in his handwriting. In fact the only time I've seen his handwriting is on some schoolwork I've read. It was so straight and tall – just like Will himself.

"There are people who study handwriting. They're called graphologists," says Nan, as if she's reading my thoughts. "I remember reading a book about it once. The way your pop rounded out all his letters showed he had a logical and sound mind. And the way he slanted his writing – a little to the right – meant that he was a sociable and outgoing sort of person who was interested in others. All good qualities in a man."

I'm thinking about Will's handwriting. I ask Nan what it means when it's straight and tall.

"Hmmm, I should think that it means he's a self-contained sort of fellow. That he's not given to extravagant shows of affection."

That's true! This is amazing!

"Is his writing small or large, would you say?" Nan asks me.

It's smaller than mine. Much smaller than Bianca's which is huge and wanders all over the place!

"Well, that says he has good concentration. That he's humble and has a good sense of himself. That he doesn't run with the pack. Anything else? Does his writing go up or down at the end?"

It's even. That's what I remember most of all. Straight across and even. It's still like that when there are no marked lines on the paper.

"Well, that means he's determined to stay on track. That his mind controls his emotions. It also means he's reliable, loyal and honest."

:-/

Reliable, loyal and honest? Well, this is where Nan has tripped up, because Will isn't *any* of those things. So much for the experts! If I was a graphologist I'd be *seriously* thinking about a new career – with everyone using computers everything looks the same now. People write all kinds of random stuff and they don't even have to sign their real names.

As we are leaving, Nan gives Mum a stack of envelopes, all addressed in her handwriting, which is almost the same as it was when she was seventeen.

"Eleanor can post those for you," says Dad. He kisses Nan goodbye and wanders off jangling the car keys.

I'm trying to remember where the Oldcastle Post Office

is. I can't ever remember having to send anything snail mail. I suppose I have to put the stamps on. How much does it cost to mail a letter anyway?

"I've almost got everything ready for the party." Mum claps her hands with excitement. "We've got the whole back room at Eugenie's restaurant and I'm getting in lovely pink cloths and the sweetest little paper lanterns. It's all going to look gorgeous. I meant to ask you, Mum, what sort of flowers would you like?"

"Roses," says Nan without any hesitation. "I'd love to have red roses."

Sunday. 5 p.m. PM. AW.

On the way back to Oldcastle in the car with Mum and
Dad, my wrecked life is slowly coming into view. Sunday
afternoon at Nan's cottage was like being in a cozy Hobbit-
hole – Bag End in The Shire. Now I'm on the road again
and heading back towards Buckingham Palace being chased
by the evil Nazgûl.

   With every landmark we pass – the statue of King
George splattered with pigeon poop, the suit of armor with
one arm missing on top of the Lionheart Dry Cleaners, and
the Princess Beatrice skate park covered with graffiti – I start
to feel more and more depressed. I know what's waiting
for me there in The Dungeon – dark creatures sent by the
all-seeing Eye of Sauron. As soon as I log on, they'll know
where I am and that scorching great eye will seek me out.

❋

"Don't forget those invites, and bring that tray of your Nan's hedgehog cake inside," says Mum, who has parked the car right up against the hedge for the millionth time. Dad and I are battling a heroic path through the thorny undergrowth when we hear Mum's strangled cry through the castle's kitchen window.

"Oh, no! Rick! Rick! Come here! NOW! We've been robbed. WE'VE BEEN ROBBED!"

Dad tears across the lawn and hurtles through the front door. I run after him, watching as bits of hedgehog cake slip over the edge of the baking tray and land on the brick path in an explosion of chocolate and desiccated coconut. Invitations flutter onto the grass.

It's a hideous scene in the family room. The cushions have been torn from the couch and thrown on the floor. The big blue-and-white Chinese pot with the palm tree in it has been pushed over and smashed. The palm fronds have been ripped off the plant and stuck in the ceiling fan. They're rotating like a crazy, giant, shredded green umbrella. Why? Who would do something like that?

All our framed family photos have been ripped down from the walls and Nan and Pop look up at me through broken glass. The vase Grandpa and Grandma Pickering gave us for Christmas has been shattered. The stuffing from the cushions is swirling in the breeze and where the TV used to be is just a bare square of nothing with some old, stale pretzels rolling around in the middle of it. How long have *they* been under there …?

"LIBBY! See what they've taken! Call the police. CALL THE POLICE!" yells Dad from the kitchen.

And then I hear Mum screech from the back of the house.

"My laptop! I left it here on the bed. It's *gone*! If they've taken my jewelry …"

Mum's laptop? I feel sick at the thought. I didn't know it was possible to feel so sick in an instant, although I should. It's what I felt when I first saw those photos of Will. And then I think *photos?* They couldn't have taken my computer and *ALL MY PHOTOS?* Not the ones I was going to print out and put in an album in a box covered in floral wrapping paper for my great-great-grandchildren?

I run through the kitchen, throwing the leftover dessert in the general direction of the counter, and race up the hall to The Dungeon. Looking at my desk I can see that where my computer used to be is just an empty patch of dust containing one amethyst stud earring. The earring I've been looking for since … MY COMPUTER HAS BEEN STOLEN!

OMG!!!! :-><

My last two and a half years of photos were on my computer! From when I started at Oldcastle High until … now.

So much history lost, as Pop said in his letter. I feel like that old church that was taken apart – stone by stone.

Mum appears in my doorway cuddling her red leather jewelry box.

"They didn't take it. Thank the Lord!" she gasps. "They got my laptop, but everything's still inside my jewelry box – my rings, my pearls, Mum's gold locket, Dad's cufflinks – they're all still here. It was boys, probably. Looking for things they could sell fast."

Mum sees my face, then my empty desk, turns and pelts back down the hall to Tilly's hovel in the South Wing. Even from there I can hear her.

"Oh, no! No, no, no! They've taken Tilly's laptop as well! Her final exams start next week! This is a *disaster!*"

All three computers are gone. Mum's business contacts and files, Tilly's schoolwork and my ENTIRE LIFE have all been stolen!

I suddenly realize that I'm now invisible. Even as I hear Dad calling with relief from the garage that his toolbox is still there, even as I see Mum running down the driveway to give Tilly the terrible news before she's out of her car.

There is no way I can ring, text, email, message or poke anyone, anywhere. For any reason. Not to deliver glad tidings or impart bad news. Not to say "I love you," "I hate you," or anything in between. Not to say "I miss you and want to see you," or "I don't and please forget I exist."

☺ ☹ :%)% :-------------) :-< :-@! :->X==|::=)) :^)oO

Everyone can forget I exist now, because I don't. I'm a ghost, haunting my own life.

I slump back on my bed and my thumping heart is the only sound in the dead silence that descends on The Dungeon.

Sunday. 7 p.m. PM. AW. PPC (post personal computer).

"Well, you're lucky they didn't take any of your valuables," says the policeman from New Oldcastle Police Station. "Looks like it was only your computers and they can easily be replaced."

Where do I start with the rank stupidity of this statement? This bloke's probably over fifty, and obviously has no idea.

"Thank goodness," says Mum, "that only last night I got the rest of the family photos off and put them on a disk. It was all this stupid business with Will on the Net that made me think of it. I can't believe I was so lucky! And Tina's got all the documents for the business on her computer too, so I'm fine."

I'm so glad that my personal tragedy has been of help to everyone! Sitting on a kitchen stool opposite me, Tilly's got her head down, her face covered by a shiny sheet of dark brown hair.

"My advice is to buy another computer as soon as you can," says the policeman. "And immediately change all your PINs and passwords to your bank accounts and suchlike. The only advice we can ever give is to back up all your data on a separate hard drive and keep that under lock and key in a safe place when you leave the house. Or take it with you. Imagine if your house was flooded or burned down?"

I've already imagined.

"Do you have contents insurance?" asks the policeman.

Dad shakes his head. "We've only got the house covered."

"Well you wouldn't be the only one; so many people find they're underinsured." The policeman shakes his head as he writes in his notepad.

I can't help feeling he enjoys telling people stuff like this.

"What we'll do is replace the TV and buy one computer that you can all share," Dad says wearily. "I'll just have to put it on the credit cards – if we're not over the limit already. Thank you, officer. We appreciate you coming over at this time on a Sunday night."

"No problem, Mr. Pickering. We'll be in touch if we hear anything. But I have to tell you we've had a rash of these kind of robberies in Oldcastle lately and it's hard to trace stolen computers. They sell easily. Well, I suppose it's a lesson learned," the policeman scolds, and puffs up his chest importantly. "Please upgrade your home security. I don't want to be here again trying to recover your wife's precious family jewelry. Good evening."

He's not even out the front door when Tilly starts to moan.

"I'm going to fail the exams! How am I going to keep studying without the Net? I start next week!"

"Well, we'll have another computer soon, and there's always the Oldcastle library," suggests Mum.

Tilly jumps to her feet and rakes her hair from her face with skinny fingers.

"The *library*?" she gasps.

She's appalled. Why wouldn't she be?

"You think I'm going to be poking around in millions of dusty books at the *library*? I haven't been there since I was five, sitting in the corner reading *The Very Hungry Caterpillar*! All my exam notes were on my computer! All my bookmarks, contacts, email addresses, photos."

"Did you back any of it up on a disk, darling?" asks Mum.

Seriously, I don't want to be around to hear Tilly's answer. Sure enough, before I can escape she starts screeching and grabbing junk off the kitchen counter and chucking it at the wall. An egg slicer bounces off the kitchen window and lands in the sink with a hideous *clang*! She throws the remains of Nan's dessert on the floor and does a crazed war dance on the top of it.

"MATILDA PICKERING! ENOUGH!"

144

Tilly is frozen with her arms in the air holding a frying pan and a spatula as we all turn to see Dad standing in the doorway.

"You will get your spoiled little bottom down to that library if that's what it takes! I will see if we have any money to buy a new computer. But we just might not. You may have heard about the Global Financial Crisis *and everything*? In the meantime, both of you ..."

Me? Why me? How come I'm included in the Tilly *Tantrum*?

"... get to your rooms! NOW!"

Tilly drops everything with clattering defiance and marches off, punching the wall in the hallway. I'm not going to argue with Dad either. I can't remember seeing him so angry. I'm about to join Tilly's parade when Dad turns on me. I should have gotten away faster.

"YOU WANT TO HAVE A GOOD THINK ABOUT ALL THE PEOPLE IN THE WORLD WHO DON'T HAVE COMPUTERS AND WHO'VE NEVER HAD ONE, MISSY," Dad roars.

Then Mum decides to chuck in her two cents.

"And what about all those poor unfortunates in refugee camps, or living on garbage piles, who haven't even got a proper roof over their heads? Most of them have never even seen a computer, let alone a telephone or had the chance to talk on one. And here's you losing three mobile phones! *Three* of them." Mum wags her finger at me.

This is so not fair! I've already been yelled at for the

whole mobile thing. I wish I could get past and go to The Dungeon, but they're both blocking the way.

Dad picks up the frying pan and bangs it down again on the counter for no good reason, making me jump with fright.

"I refuse to be held ransom by some idiotic invention called the World Wide Web!" Dad rages. "I promise you that if every last computer on earth was dumped down the garbage, life would still go on and the world would be a better place for it ..."

"Now, Rick, that's going a bit far ..." says my mother, who thankfully has stepped in as a human shield. "There's a lot of diseases in the world that have been cured by doctors using computers, and then there are all other kinds of scientific research that ..."

"I GREW UP WITHOUT A COMPUTER IN THE HOUSE, AND I DID JUST FINE!" Dad interrupts. "I knew how to look up things in the encyclopedia. I read books. I asked my mother and father how to do stuff. And what about this financial mess the world's in? I can guarantee there would be less thievery and greediness if people had to talk to each other face-to-face instead of just sending emails and texts and garbage."

I manage to duck out and avoid the rest of the lecture on the Days Before Computers Were Invented. BTW, when was the computer invented? I realize that I have absolutely no idea, and without my computer, no way to look it up.

But I have to wonder, if I didn't have a computer or a mobile phone, would I still have Will? I can feel the tears rushing towards me again as The Dungeon door clunks behind me.

Monday. 9 a.m. PM. AW. PPC.

Today as I drag myself up the school steps, I notice how many people are almost walking into the flagpole as they concentrate on typing their last-minute texts.

Who are they talking to? What are they saying?

SKL now, See U LTR.
s4mvl8r
Huh?
Gotta go. Catch U.
SISDU
SPYS
SOZ?
AYT?

There are billions of these messages swirling in the air – a constant, invisible, whirling tornado of vowels, consonants, question and exclamation marks.

EEEK. LOL. HAHA! ROFL. OMGGGGG!

My mobile's been gone more than a week and I've noticed that my fingers have stopped straying without my permission and given up trying to tap on an imaginary keypad. This morning my hands are all mine and I stop to pick one of the first gardenias of the season from the glossy dark-green bushes that crowd the front steps of Oldcastle High. I pin it on my navy blue blazer pocket – just above my broken heart.

A sign outside the principal's office warns that mobiles are forbidden in class, but most of us push the rule to the max. We're always *buzzing* and texting under the desks. It sounds pretty sexy, until you see that it's Jai who's the main offender. When you see a huddle of bodies at the back of the room it's a sure sign that Jai's found a YouTube clip of a surfer being savaged by a shark or some psycho raving on about something weird – usually wearing a balaclava and waving an AK-47!

Today as I walk across the quad, everyone's looking at me sideways since I'm the latest loony to make a spectacle of herself on the World Wide Web. I hate what Will's done to me and I don't think I'll ever recover from the humiliation, but something Carmelita wrote keeps going around and around in my head – that I should have worked it out with

Will *in private*.

Too late now.

Everyone in school laughing at him – and me – as they follow every gory detail of our break-up online is not something I ever wanted. And even though I know Will probably deserves to be made a fool of, I also remember what Nan said – that he's a *self-contained sort of fellow.* He must be hating this even more than me. I'll bet his dad has told him that it serves him right.

And it does serve him right. If what I saw is true. Photos can't lie. Can they?

I'm approaching the northwest terrace when Tenzin Choepel, a boy from my year, jumps out from behind a pillar.

"Good morning, Elly!" he says, with the biggest, dazzling white smile that almost splits his handsome brown face in half.

Tenzin's family is from Tibet. They came here to Oldcastle three years ago. I know his story well because I interviewed him for the March edition of the *Posh Post* – the month that marked the fiftieth anniversary of the occupation of Tibet by the Chinese.

His mother and father escaped their country sixteen years ago by hiding in the back of a truck under some boxes of engine parts and were really lucky not to be found by the Chinese guards at the border. From there they had to cross a river by pulling themselves hand-over-hand on ropes in the middle of the night. They made it to Katmandu and from there to the Tibetan refugee camp in Dharamsala in India where the government-in-exile rules. It's where the Dalai Lama lives and it's where Tenzin and his sisters were born.

Tenzin's named after the Dalai Lama. He's a Buddhist and, even after everything his family's been through, he's always smiling.

"I've heard that you are ... er ... Would you like to go to the dance with me?" he asks.

I should be flattered, I suppose, but right now his invitation makes me burst into tears. I run away from him down the concrete terrace, wiping my eyes with the sleeve of my blazer.

Tenzin probably looked at my FacePlace and read that I was the happiest girl in the world without Will.

I hate this! I hate that anyone would think that our relationship meant so little to me. I hate that people think I'll go out with any old fish in the sea. I hate that everyone thinks they know about my life. I hate that I let Tilly talk me into putting that stupid page on the Net!

I should have walked down to the beach at sunset and thrown a single red rose into the surf. It would have been a private funeral. Just something between me and my own bruised heart.

I'm hiding under a stairwell and trying to get my act together when I see Bianca barreling towards me at a million miles an hour. Her hair comes at me first. She's totally teased and sprayed her do, and this morning it looks like the nest of a golden orb-weaver spider.

"Elly! Elly!" shrieks Bianca. "Why didn't you call me over the weekend?"

I patiently explain to her what I have already explained – that I don't have a phone.

"But you could have gotten in touch with me eye2eye."

I explain that I haven't got a computer either.

"Huh?" says Bianca.

This information does not make sense to Bianca. *It does not compute.*

"But, but … you could have …" Bianca is stopped in her tracks and cocks her head on the side like a confused chicken.

She can't imagine what it would be like not to have her phone in her hand. In fact, even as she's talking to me she's texting someone else. Truly, Bianca's a genius at this stuff and I can only imagine that when she leaves school she'll be an air traffic controller.

"Anyway," Bianca chirps. "Just so you know … Jayden's on the warpath. He read Lily's FacePlace, and yours, and he's gonna *smash* Will! If he's down at Wobbegong or Hammerhead or Gummy this afternoon Will's seriously gonna get it."

Bianca shifts her schoolbag from shoulder to shoulder and hops from one foot to the other. The adrenaline's pumping and I don't think I've ever seen her so excited. Then Jai turns up at her elbow. His grin reminds me of a crumbed prawn.

"Yeah. Will's goin' down," he squeaks.

This is SO BAD! I would never in a trillion years want anyone to physically hurt Will. I might have called him a love rat, but if they think that I would be pleased to see Will smashed they've got rocks in their heads. I tell Jai to tell Jayden to LAY OFF!

"Too bad," sneers Jai. "Will should of thought of all that before he put the moves on Lily. What happened after they got out of the spa is what Jay'd like to know."

The pathetic slimeball! I'm still holding onto the vital information that Jai has been hassling Lily too, according to Tilly – who heard it from Georgie – who heard it from Lily herself. Will there ever be a right time to tell Bianca? At the moment she'd just laugh it off and think I was making it up.

Again I warn Jai that Jayden had better not try anything. Or else. Or else what? Who can I tell? That officer from Oldcastle police who didn't understand anything about anything? I can hear myself: *Some boys are planning something, somewhere – so Jai told me ...*

Bianca and Jai put their empty heads together, creating a wind tunnel, and then they run off. I watch as they both yap away on their phones.

That's it!

<u>Bianca is now officially my ex-BF.</u>

I have to warn Will. He can't go down to the beach tonight! The school bell rings and as I run along the terrace I am praying for massive onshore winds to blow the sea as flat and shiny as a mirror.

* ❋ *

In class I'm watching as people text each other under their desks. I suppose that in Dad's day a folded note would have been passed from hand to hand.

OOOH! BIG RUMBLE DOWN ON THE BEACH TONIGHT. BE THERE OR BE SQUARE!

I'm phone-free, so I've got no part in it. I'm above it all. It's odd – like I'm looking down on everything that's happening from the calm, sunny eye of the storm. But swirling around me there's a current of violent emotion that will catch up with Will unless I warn him.

In English Mr. York asks me how my work is going on the *Posh Post*. As a matter of fact it's not going anywhere. At all. Not since my computer was nicked last night.

"Hmmm, yes, well," he says. "The October edition's due out in a couple of days and it will count for your final exam mark, so in that case you'll have to work on it from the school's computer center. You'd better get over there now."

Groan! I'll be in there with all the tinys from Year Seven doing their dumb projects on the breeding cycle of frogs. Ribbit!

Soon enough I'm sitting in a scuzzy portable classroom

next to the school shop trying to get some sense from a computer that is so old it was last used by velociraptors in Jurassic Park.

Waiting for stuff to download seems to take for-ev-er. And while I wait there's only Karen Crenshaw to talk to. Karen's genius with all kinds of technology, but hasn't quite gotten the hang of elastic bands. She has crazy, tiny pigtails sprouting from all over her head. It looks like a cushion losing its stuffing.

To pass the time, Karen tells me that her mum is getting their kitchen renovated. By the time the stuff I want finally appears on the screen, I have been informed in excruciating detail that the new Crenshaw kitchen will feature fake marble countertops and a barbecue with hot rocks. (YAWN!)

Finally, the info is downloaded and I fiddle around with a few articles submitted for the *Posh Post*. As usual they're all from boring teachers who want to inform the entire school of their great and good works.

Worm Farm for 7A – Let's Get Wriggling!

Year Eight Goes Eco-Troppo – Our Afternoon at the Gummy Beach Environment Center!

By the time I edit all this earth-shattering information, it's almost lunchtime. The smell of meat and pastry wafting from the school shop pie warmer is making Karen twitch and me feel slightly ill – although that's probably as much from the thought of speaking to Will as it is from the stench of curried meat. The bell rings for lunchtime and she's out the door like a rocket, clutching her $2.50 in her sweaty palm.

Now that no one's watching I can drop in on any website I like. FacePlace is where I should start, but what's the use? There will only be more nasty stuff on there aimed at me and Will.

Maybe Sun Tzu can tell me how I've come to be caught up in this battle? What went wrong? After all, my enemy was Jai. How did I end up sacrificing Will? Why does it feel like I'm losing everything?

In *The Art of War* I find there are "five dangerous faults which may affect a general" (and lead you to being bombed into submission).

Looking at the list I can see that I am totally guilty of the first four sins – recklessness, cowardice, a hasty temper and a delicacy of honor. Will told me not to take any notice of Jai's stupid insults. If I hadn't been so *delicate* I wouldn't have cared. Maybe I shouldn't have been such a *coward* and confronted Jai. Instead, I let my *temper* lead me into being *reckless*.

The fifth sin is an "over solicitude" for one's men. Huh?

solicitude |səˈlisətjud|
noun care or concern for someone or something.

I think this means that I have been more worried about Bianca's broken heart than my own. I should have told her about Jai going behind her back as soon as I knew. Maybe then I'd still have Will. I can't put this off any longer. Even though my stomach is bouncing like a basketball, I have to go see Will.

✳

Of course I know where Will will be this sunny afternoon – down back, under the jacaranda tree. It's his place of refuge. Even Jayden's not so stupid as to try to bash him up inside the school grounds.

I peer around the corner of the school shop and see him in the distance, just sitting there on the grass. It's like my heart's being squeezed by the claw of a dying crab. I can hardly breathe. Will's curly blond head is bent over a book. I watch as he looks up through the branches and then falls back. He's lying with his long legs stretched out and he looks like he doesn't have a care in the world. Maybe he hasn't. Maybe he's thinking about Lily.

I take a deep breath. I'll walk along the side fence where I'm not in plain view. I feel like some kind of ridiculous crazed stalker as I dart between the trees. I'm now as close as I can be without being seen, and I reckon there's only about twenty yards of open ground between him and where I'm hiding behind this stinking dumpster. I smooth my skirt and scrape the hair from my face with my headband. One last breath, I look around the corner and …

It's Lily!

She's walking up to Will. He sees her and jumps to his feet and runs his hands through his golden curls. Of course he'll be with Lily! *I'm so stupid!* Of course he's with her under the jacaranda tree. It's where we always used to meet every lunchtime.

It's weird though. He's backing away and turns his head as she keeps coming towards him. And now she stops and gets something out of her bag and holds it out to him. It's an envelope. He's shaking his head, he doesn't want to take it, but she insists. She's holding it out to him and I can see her pleading. Finally he takes it from her and puts it in his blazer pocket.

Now they're talking and both their heads are bowed. She's wiping her eyes and it looks like she's crying. He's shaking his head and shuffling his feet. Then he steps forward and takes her in his arms and …

I'm running. Flying back down the side fence. I can hear someone moaning in pain and I realize that it's me.

Monday. 2 p.m.
PM. AW. PPC.

This afternoon I can barely see the desk in front of me.
Tears spill and plop on the open page of my book. I'm
hiding behind my hair and I've managed not to let anyone
see. I don't want anyone's sympathy. It's my fault this time
that I'm feeling so pathetic. I was bound to see Will and
Lily together in person, but I wasn't prepared to see them
like that so soon. In each other's arms. I'm only thankful that
I didn't see them kiss.

If I had my mobile right now I'd ring that stupid number
where you can text two names and see if they're a match.
Only I probably don't have to. Will was right, our techno
lives are just a mirage. I saw with my own eyes that Will and
Lily go together – fair hair, dark hair; gray eyes, black eyes;

tanned skin, pale skin. I didn't need a mobile phone to tell me that. At least I probably saved myself $1.50.

I can't believe I ever thought that I should be the one to warn Will. *I'm so idiotic!* I should have thought it through and known that Lily was there to care for him. He's hers now. She's his now. And their fates have nothing to do with me anymore. They're holding hands and swimming away together in an open sea.

And this little leg rope is untied, slack and all out of bounce.

We're with Mrs. Ferguson for Drama. An assignment about the films and television series of *Jane Eyre* by Charlotte Brontë is plonked in front of me. As part of our study guide she hands us a list of websites to look at. Hah!

I happily inform Fergie that I don't have a computer anymore, so this assignment will be impossible for me to complete. (Even though I happen to be reading Tilly's copy of *Jane Eyre* at the moment. I started a few weeks ago after Mum and I watched the series on TV and ended up blubbering wrecks. Of course I'm not about to tell Fergie that.)

"There's always the school computer center, Elly," she sniffs, and reties her floral scrunchie around her red ponytail. "And of course there's the library. Remember *the library?* It's where they keep *books*."

Everyone giggles and I mutter at the sarcastic old bag under my breath.

"Jane Eyre didn't have a computer and still managed to

gain an education. So I'm sure you will too. In fact—" she stops in her tracks, suddenly in the grip of a brilliant idea.

Uh-oh! Everyone ducks their heads, expecting a battering.

"I'd like everyone to follow Ms. Pickering's lead," she announces from the front of the room. "You can all consult the library for this assignment and complete a part of your research from the extensive volumes contained therein on English history, culture, literature and cinema."

There is a huge groan from the room as Fergie's brainstorm unleashes its full power.

"I will expect a full bibliography at the end of your work. I'll inform Mrs. Wales at the library desk that each one of you will be visiting and borrowing reference books over the next week. I will also contact the Oldcastle library and leave a full list of all your names so you can check in there as well. This will be a *wonderful* experiment. It will give you a true insight into what it was like to gain an education In The Days Before …"

I look around the room and see that every single person is staring at me, wanting to wring my neck with their bare hands. I feel so low that I want to stand up and ask who'd like to go first? *All righty! Everyone get in line!*

There's a *thwack!* on the back of my head and I turn to see that Jai's just lobbed a half-eaten doughnut at me. Bianca looks utterly furious. Oh, well, as they say, every cloud has a silver lining – or in this case, strawberry icing.

Monday. 3:20 p.m.
PM. AW. PPC.

Tilly pulls up in her battered, old silver Mazda outside the school gates. She's offered me a lift home and I'm so grateful I don't have to take the bus and face everyone from Year Nine paying out on me. I jump in and she roars into the traffic on Charles Drive without signaling. The car behind us toots angrily and she holds up one elegant finger.

"BOG OFF, YOU FOOL!" Tilly shouts at the rearview mirror. Then she turns to me and I can see her cheeks are pink with fury.

"By the way, we're not going straight home," she fumes. "I have to go to the Oldcastle *library!* The *actual* library! As if I'm in some third world country or something. I tell you, if Dad doesn't come home tonight with a new computer, I'm

going to *lose* it! I told him. I can't buy myself a new one.
I haven't got enough cash. This is my *future* we're talking
about. I've only got a week till I start my exams and I've lost
all my study notes."

I want to tell Tilly that I saw Will and Lily together today.
I open my mouth to speak, but she's off again.

"And I get down to the school library this afternoon
to do some research and it's totally clogged with pathetic
dweebs from Year Nine all making a racket! How did that
happen?"

Of course, as a pathetic dweeb from Year Nine, I know
exactly how that happened. I better not say it was my fault
everyone's gone there to do their assignments. Tilly weaves
back into the other lane and there's another angry toot.

"WHAT AM I? INVISIBLE?!" she yells out the window.

By now I am gripping the door handle, clinging like a
mollusk on a rock in a tsunami.

"I've gotta get to a computer!" Tilly complains. "I need
peace and quiet. I have to finish this presentation on the
International Space Station. And do you think I can find that
in a *book?* Hardly! Technology's moving at a million miles an
hour! Books are so slow, they're not even snail. They're still
trying to wriggle their way out of some primordial swamp!
Do you think there would even be an International Space
Station if we only had *books?*"

Tilly brakes so hard that my schoolbag comes flying over
from the back seat and smashes into the windshield. I grab it

so at least I can see what we're about to hit.

"You know something, Elly?" says Tilly.

No. I don't know anything ... except that sitting in this car going at a million miles an hour I wish Tilly was watching the road instead of boring her eyes into mine.

"All the *idiots* – Mum and Dad and teachers and everyone else included – who think that the Internet is scrambling our brains *Just. Do. Not. Get. It.* They're evolutionary throwbacks," shouts Tilly, as she slaps the steering wheel. "They're no better than the flat-earth morons who locked up Galileo for daring to think the earth revolved around the sun.

"It makes me *so* mad and I am sick up to *here* ..." and she slashes her throat with a murderous gesture, "with their dumb, endless lectures about the way life *used* to be. I wish they would just SHUT UP! The rest of us are trying to *think*."

But, I say to Tilly, I can't help wondering whether it's the Internet that broke my heart. She instantly swivels her head to me, even though she should really be concentrating on the semi-trailer in front.

"I'll tell you something," she says passionately. "All the technology in the world can't break your heart. It's humans and their Neanderthal emotions that break your heart. The only thing that happened is that you found out Will was two-timing you a lot faster and more easily than you might have when Mum and Dad were our age. It doesn't alter the fact that you deserve a boyfriend better than Will. It doesn't mean he's not a liar and a cheat. Think of the alternative

– what if Will was carrying on with Lily behind your back for ages and you didn't know?"

I nod. She's right. Everyone's right – Mum and Dad, Nan, Tilly, Carmelita, Bianca and Jai, Jayden, Lily, Georgie … everyone's right … and everyone's wrong. Problem is, I don't know the difference between right and wrong anymore. My brain's like a busted GPS – heading off in all directions.

"The Internet is mankind's greatest invention!" Tilly declares. "Bigger than the wheel or the telephone. There are more than a billion people who can talk to each other and share their lives and opinions. And we're all part of the best conversation the world's ever had."

Oh yeah? I ask how come most of the conversation on the Net seems to be about Angelina Jolie's kids.

"Don't be smart, Eleanor," snaps Tilly.

She's called me "Eleanor" and that hardly happens, so she must be about to give me a serious talking to.

"It's exactly like real life," says my sister, who seems to have been blessed with X-ray vision as she narrowly misses a biker who's shaking his leather fist at us. "You meet someone down the street and say, 'Hey, what about Angelina Jolie's kids?' But when you get past that, there's a whole lot more stuff to talk about. Big stuff. Important stuff. And that's what most of us are doing on the Net. All the rest is just dumb gossip."

Tilly's phone rings and I sincerely hope she's not going

to answer it while she's driving. No such luck. She rummages in her handbag and again we veer across the road to jeering toots from other cars. She scans the screen and now she's texting, driving and talking all at the same time. It's utterly nerve-racking.

"Do you know that right this minute I could probably send a text from my mobile phone to the International Space Station circling almost 350 miles above the earth?" she says.

I tell her what Mum said about all the people in refugee camps dragging buckets of water. If they had a mobile, what would they ask the International Space Station? *Hey, can you see my cardboard shack from up there?*

"Of course there are millions who live in poverty right now," Tilly nods. "But it's not the Internet that's causing it. One day every single person in the world will be online and have unlimited access to all the knowledge that's stored there, just like us." We fly into the library's parking lot, brakes squealing. "And they won't have to spend three hours looking for a parking space to get to it."

❋

"I'm sorry, dear, but you can't get on the Net today. All the computers have been booked for this afternoon and right through to this evening," says the woman from behind the front desk at the Oldcastle library.

I look at Tilly and see the blood drain from her face.

"What?" She shakes her head, uncomprehending, as if the librarian is speaking Swahili.

"We only have four computers in operation at the moment. Of course you're very welcome to bring your laptop in and use our wireless network ..."

The rest of her sentence trails away as Tilly rudely turns her back and marches out the door, stopping only to kick over the Wilderness Society plaster koala on the sidewalk. The librarian's mouth is hanging open in shock and before she can complain about Tilly's appallingly bad manners, I quickly ask her when a computer might become available.

"Any time between 9 a.m. and about 4 p.m. is perfectly fine," she says. "But I don't suppose that's much help to you, being during school hours."

She's right there. I thank her and race across the parking lot to where Tilly is already backing her car out. I leap in the passenger seat and with a screech of tires we roar out onto the main road again.

"I need an Internet café. There's one down at Crowns on Wobbegong Beach," Tilly gabbles, as she puts the foot down.

Wobbegong Beach? Erk! If I could turn this car around right now, I would. Could Will be there? Could he be there with Lily? Could Bianca, Jai and Jayden – and in fact most of Year Nine – be there lying in wait behind a tea tree with a lump of wood? If I had my mobile I'd be able to ring Bianca and find out. I suppose Tilly would lend me her phone, but now that Ponsford The Airhead is off my Christmas card list, there's no way I'm calling her.

As Winchester Headland comes into view at a truly terrifying speed, my schoolbag turns into a safety airbag. I whine to Tilly that I want to go home.

"You can catch the bus back if you want," says Tilly grimly. "I've got a ton of stuff to print out and I've got to get organized. I start exams next week, Elly. Next week! That's seven days away. Stop being so selfish."

The car comes to a stop on the gravel with another almighty lurch and I'm saved by my bag from catapulting through the windshield and onto the pavement. Tilly's out the door in a flash. I sit and catch my breath and peer through the car windows in all directions. There's no one around. The coast is literally clear, so I climb out of the car.

The first thing I'm glad to see is that there's absolutely no surf. The sun is mostly hidden behind banks of gray clouds and the sea is choppy and dull. Here and there the odd whitecap is being whipped up by a cross-shore wind. As Will would say, *It's blown out and messy – nothing to see here.*

That means of course that Will won't be down at the beach tonight, and I hope he's home in his cozy little shack in Hammerhead. At least that's one place Jayden wouldn't dare go. Will's dad Took would bounce him down the sand on his pointy head.

But then I can't help wondering whether Lily is there too. Is she sitting on the floor with Pookie playing Boggle? Is she dipping into jars of glaze, helping Jasmine decorate her pretty pots? Or is she sitting on the old cane couch in Will's bedroom, snuggled in his arms, her head on his chest and watching the late afternoon sun slant across the ocean?

The thought that Lily might have slipped so easily into my place, eating Jasmine's delicious curry puffs and listening to and laughing at Took's crazy stories, makes me unbearably sad. I wish I had my mobile now. I'd ring Carmelita. I know she'd say, *It's all in your imagination, Els. Just calm down and stay focused on what you know.*

But I don't have my mobile this afternoon and I'm alone with thoughts that take flight like a sea eagle, swooping off towards the misty horizon.

I button up my blazer to keep myself warm and think back to lunchtime today for the trillionth time. I can't stop replaying the scene in my head. What was in that envelope Lily held out to Will? The one he didn't want to take. A love letter? And why was she crying? I'm still trying to imagine what could have gone down there when there's a loud *bang!* from the front door of Crown's. I see Tilly – her dark eyebrows scrunched together like two demented caterpillars – stomping towards the car.

"STUPID BACKPACKERS!" she spits, and wrenches open the door. "Stealing our waves and hogging our computers! Get in the car!"

And then we're backing out and skidding on gravel.

"You should have seen those boofheads huddled over

169

every single screen in the place with their cans of Red Bull
and bags of jelly beans and disgusting knitted beanies.
Playing their lame online games. Poncing around pretending
to be dragon slayers or wizards ... it's all dumb, time-wasting
GARBAGE!"

So much for the great online meeting of brainiacs in the
sky.

"What am I going to do *now?*" wails Tilly. "It's all so ..."

And, uh-oh! Tilly's crying! As I watch, the tears spring
from her eyes with such force they land and *ping* off the
steering wheel.

"I'll drop you home and then go to Eddie's place," she
sniffs. "I'll use his laptop. I think the place upstairs has wireless
and I might be able to use it if I can get the password. But
there's no printer ... so I guess I'll use a memory stick. And
then print it out tomorrow ... at school or the library ... This is
a *nightmare!*"

It is a bad dream. We're teenagers on the edge of a
technological breakdown. And if we're this hopeless and
unable to cope without our shiny gadgets, imagine if we
were caught in a war zone, invaded by aliens or about to be
hit by an asteroid?

EEEK! That wasn't an asteroid that almost wiped us out,
but a Beefeater Butchery van. I beg Tilly to *pleeeeease* slow
down. She pretends not to hear how terrified I am as we
whiz along Kensington Street. I suddenly remember that the
post office is meant to be here somewhere. In the schoolbag

I'm hugging to my chest there's a pile of Nan's party
invitations that I promised to post.

Monday. 8 p.m.
PM. AW. PPC.

I.S.O.L.A.T.E. Isolate. By my calculation, with double word score and this word here ... it's 47 points. We're sitting at the dining table tonight playing Scrabble and I really can't remember the last time we did this.

"Hmmm, nice score," says Mum. "I think you've got me beaten, you little beast! You've got a way with words. I was never going to be a match for you."

I laugh. I actually laugh. Can you believe that Mum and I are sitting together in our PJs scoffing a king-size bar of chocolate? And we haven't fought once? Maybe this is life Post Personal Computer. Instead of Mum being on her laptop in the kitchen and me being on FacePlace in The Dungeon, we've spent the last two hours putting kiwifruit

172

yogurt treatments on each other's hair and playing board games.

"Your Nan's a champion player," says Mum, as she tucks a gloopy strand of hair under her plastic wrap turban. "Oh, and by the way, did you get those party invitations off?"

I tell Mum that I'll do it straight after school tomorrow.

"Thanks, darling. We have to remember that a lot of elderly people like to have plenty of notice about their social engagements. They'll all want to write an RSVP and post it to your grandmother."

I know what ROFL means, but what's RSVP?

"Répondez, s'il vous plaît!" Mum sings, as she breaks off a massive hunk of chocolate and stuffs it into her mouth. She's obviously happy to be telling me something I don't know. "It's French."

I think that's what she said anyway. It's hard to tell through that gobful of hazelnut crunch.

"It means that when you send an invitation you are also asking people to 'answer, please.'"

Yeah, but why is it in French?

"Because the French have always been considered, throughout history, to have set the standard for manners," says Mum, spraying me with bits of soggy, half-chewed nut.

The French set the standard for manners? As if! What about that whole nuclear testing in the South Pacific thing that we studied in history last week?

"Yes, apart from that," Mum smiles, swallows and goes for the coconut ice. "You and your sister are so smart. How am I ever supposed to keep up?"

I'm not as smart as she thinks. I mumble this to Mum as I take the square of Turkish delight that she knows is my fave. Without my mobile and computer I'm feeling dumber than I ever have.

"Well, I wouldn't look at it that way, Elly," says Mum. "Everything you need to know is right there in that big brain and that big heart of yours. You have to listen to what your intuition tells you. You often can't hear the voice within when it's drowned out by the millions of opinions around you, but as your pop always said, *To thine own self be true.*"

Yeah, but what if you don't even know who "thine self" is? I wish that I could go to www.thineownself.com, answer a simple questionnaire and be on my way.

"And you, my girl," says Mum, "are a good and kind person, so don't forget that."

We are packing up the Scrabble set when Dad finally walks in the door. He's really late. He's bent over and looks as if he is carrying the whole weight of Ascot Couriers on his broad back.

"Eight gone," he sighs. He dumps his backpack and slumps into a kitchen chair. "They sacked eight blokes today. It's the Global Financial Crisis."

"Oh, no!" Mum exclaims and then sinks into a chair

next to him.

"I've just come from the pub," Dad sighs. "Everyone's worried about the future. I feel for the blokes with young families and everything."

This time I know what *and everything* means. It means being unemployed and not being able to afford mortgage payments and school fees and the fact that it will be hard to find another job. I've started to see a lot of "closing down sale" signs in shop windows around Britannia.

"Rick, could you be next to go?" whispers Mum.

"Yep. Management has assured me that I've got a job till Christmas, but after that, who knows?"

Ulp! Now the *and everything* also includes my new mobile phone and computer! And then I feel bad about thinking that. Tilly's right, I should stop being so selfish.

I watch as Mum and Dad squeeze hands and look at each other silently for what feels like a very long time. Then Mum's up on her feet and pacing.

"Well, we'll just have to watch every cent, that's all," she says with determination, as she pulls tight the belt on her leopard-print, fake-fur dressing gown.

"I've still got quite a lot of events booked. People might be cutting back on how much money they spend, but they're still getting married and celebrating life. They won't stop doing that."

"I hope you're right," says Dad morosely.

"And," Mum continues, "we'll economize. It'll do us all

good. Elly, you can start doing some extra cooking – no more take out! I might lose a bit of weight."

Mum slaps her tummy and the sound is actually a bit more gruesome than she might have expected – like leftover lasagna in a trash bag. Mum pretends she hasn't heard and keeps on.

"Tilly? Well, she'll have to knuckle down and take a few more shifts at Earl's so she can put the money towards a new laptop."

I know I probably shouldn't – but I *have* to ask about getting my new computer and mobile. Dad's not impressed.

"No. No way," he says and his hand chops the air as if he is trying to break a brick with a karate move. "We'll get your mother a new laptop and you'll all have to share."

I'm sensible enough not to go on with it, but the idea of the three of us sharing a computer is an utter fantasy. Hmmm.

Maybe I can help Mum with a few of her events and earn some money that way? Then at least I could buy myself a new mobile.

"Well ..." Mum looks at Dad. "What do you think, Rick?"

"If she can make herself useful, I don't see why not. You won't ever hire a quicker learner than Elly."

"I could do with a hand," agrees Mum. "So yes, Miss Eleanor Elizabeth Pickering, you are Regal Events' first apprentice! I'll pay you $10 an hour."

And that's how I come to spend the rest of the night sorting white and silver candied almonds into tiny tulle bags and tying them with silky white ribbons – and make $25!

Tuesday. 4:30 p.m.
AM. PM. PPC.

Finally! I get to 25 Buckingham Street after trudging from the bus stop. The weather has changed and it's really warm. It feels like mid-summer instead of mid-spring and I'm loaded down with a million bags and books.

Our mailbox is cringe-making! Dad had it made in the shape of a golden royal carriage pulled by four tin horses with plumes on their foreheads, which are now scungy and half-chewed by possums. I sort through the usual pile of bills and furniture catalogs that have been stuffed into the carriage. *Blah, blah, blah!*

And then I see an Express Post letter addressed to me. I tear it open and inside – OMG! – there's an envelope addressed to me. Not some stupid advertising thingo or a catalog, but a real letter addressed to *Ms. E. Pickering*. Turning over the back, I see it's from: *C. Martinez, Toledo Nut Farm, Mooloowah.*

Carmelita has actually written me a letter! I carefully unstick the flap of the envelope and there's a whiff of gardenia perfume. Even the notepaper is decorated with pictures of gardenias.

Hello beautiful girl!

Who would have thought I would ever write you a letter? I sent a crucial eye2eye on Sunday and didn't hear anything. I know you don't have a mobile, so I thought I might as well do the old-fashioned thing and write.

Do you like the notepaper? I always remember that you love gardenias. (I put some of Mum's Chanel gardenia eau de toilette in here!) Mum says she'll send this express post and it will get to you tomorrow (Tuesday). That's exceptionally fast, dontcha reckon?

I wanted to tell you the BIG news. I am coming to Oldcastle! Truly!

The family is coming down on Friday afternoon to see my Auntie Isabella for her birthday party on Saturday afternoon. And that means I can come to the dance with you on Sat. night.

I know I won't have a date, but, hey, who cares? Maybe you can be my date?

I'm desperate to see you, so I'll come over to yours on
Friday night at about 7 pm. OK?
Write back, or call any time.
Love ya,
Carmelita XOXOXOXOXO

P.S: I have enclosed some pics of Viscount the pig.
Looking great, dontcha reckon?

Yahoo! This is the *best* news, ever! This is my first letter,
ever! And how good does Viscount look – for a pig!

Inside the Palace I dump all the stuff I have bought to
make dinner tonight – frozen (well, it *was* frozen) puff pastry,
ground beef, garlic, onions, peas and curry powder. I'm
going to make curry puffs. I watched Jasmine make them
often enough and I can't go wrong.

And then in the delicious cool shade of the empty kitchen,
with no one home except me, Camilla and Harry, I pour
myself an icy cranberry juice and let myself think about Will.

Today has been an extraordinary day.

The journey of a thousand miles starts with one step. So says
one of Mum's inspirational writings she's stuck on the fridge
under a frangipani magnet. So let's start with my first step
into the quad this morning.

Imagine the scene: It's a calm and clear, sunny Tuesday
when Bianca runs at me, full bore. I see that her hair,
weirdly, is as flat as the Nullarbor Plain – with what looks

like the odd clump of spiky spinifex grass sticking up. (Without my expertise, Bianca's hair is always going to look like a disaster area and this gives me some satisfaction.)

"You won't guess what, Elly!" she squeals, as she takes my arm in a wrestling hold and pushes me behind some trash cans on the terrace outside the first-aid room.

Try me. I'm beyond guessing. I couldn't have predicted anything that's happened to me over the past eleven days.

"LILY AND JAYDEN ARE BACK TOGETHER," shouts Bianca, her blue eyes wide with the thrill of this information.

Whaaaa? Honestly. This is the last thing I was expecting.

I see the school nurse, Mrs. Parker Bowles, scowling at us through the Venetian blinds and mouthing at us to keep the noise down. How can anyone be sick at this hour of the morning? Unless it's one of Mrs. Ferguson's "morning migraines" (AKA hangovers).

"It's so true. They are going together again," crows Bianca. "Jai told me last night after school. That's why none of us went chasing Will down at the beach last night. Jayden told everyone that Lily told him, to tell us, to lay off – so we did."

I remember the hideous car trip last night with Tilly and the time I spent looking out for Will, not to mention the torturous hours imagining him and Lily together. If I'd had a mobile, Bianca would have told me the latest and I would have been saved all that brain cell trauma.

Hold on. Did Lily dump Will? Or did Will dump Lily? Or is there something else I should be thinking about?

Why were both of them so sad under the jacaranda tree yesterday? I just can't figure it out and I'm sure that Bianca doesn't have the first clue.

"I know *everything*!" she declares.

I see dozens of shiny, jeweled bracelets slide down from under the sleeve of her white shirt and over her wrist to where her busy fingers are tracing the keypad of her mobile. Am I holding her up from something? Even as she's talking to me she's imagining who she might talk to next.

"What happened was, Lily crawled back to Jayden because she realized Will just wasn't good enough for her. Will's kind of weird and doesn't have that many friends. He was desperate to get a girlfriend as cool and popular as Lily, but in the end ..."

IN THE END HE COULD ONLY GET SOMEONE AS UNCOOL AND UNPOPULAR AS *ME*?

Is that what Bianca's saying?

If I could tip my water bottle onto her empty yellow-carpeted head, I reckon Bianca would screech: *I'm melting. I'm melting!* She'd end up a steaming yellow-greenish puddle under the trash cans.

"No! No! What I meant was ..." Bianca stutters and trips and fumbles and ...

Bing-bong! She's saved by the bell. Lucky for her!

"Anyway, see you after school," she trills. "We're all going to Palatial Pizzas again ... I was going to say I'll ring you, but you haven't got a mobile so ..."

Oh, what a shame that Bianca won't be able to reach me. I'm so sorry I won't be able to sit there trying to imagine which pizza Jai reminds me of. But I'll have a guess – a Jumbo Scumbag Special with extra anchovies!

❋

For the rest of the day I couldn't concentrate on anything. At lunch I peered around the corner of the school shop again and saw Will under the jacaranda tree. He was talking with Bombie Logan – one of his surfing mates. Bianca's talking total garbage. Will's got heaps of friends – he just doesn't choose to hang with most of the dead heads at Bogan Central Oldcastle High, that's all.

I wanted to go and see him with every tiny atom of my body, but maybe what Bianca said was right, and Will's already moved on. Which is, sadly, what I have to do too.

Later I was walking past the field and saw Lily and Jayden sitting way out there in the middle by themselves, their heads together, so I knew what Bianca said about them being back together was true at least.

Would I want Will back if I could have him? If he asked me? My heart said "yes" but my head said "no." My stomach couldn't give me an answer and turned end-over-end all afternoon.

Of course what Bianca said chewed away at me all day, like little teeth gnawing at my elbow. (She really does remind me of a guinea pig.) Am I really uncool and unpopular?

So this afternoon, sitting at the kitchen counter, I pick up Carmelita's letter and re-read it. I love her gorgeous handwriting. It slants a little bit to the right, the letters are rounded and even and she decorates some of them with curly bits. I'm no graphologist, but I'll bet it means she is a generous, thoughtful and kind person, because that's what she is.

She's always been there for me. Even back at Big-Ears Day Care she'd have given me her blankie if I'd needed it. I've always been cool with her and she's all the friends I need in the world in one.

I unpack all my shopping and start on my curry puffs. One sneaky part of me is thinking that if Will and I ever did get back together, I could make him curry puffs. And then I realize that, despite all the lectures I've had, I'm still a total doormat – or should I say, a limp sheet of puff pastry.

And then I remember – I still haven't posted Nan's invitations!

Tuesday. 5:30 p.m.
PM. AW. PPC.

I'm standing in Kensington Street, outside the post office.
Weirdly enough it's right here in between Footman Shoes
and Excellency Hardware and I've never noticed it.

Pushing through the front door, I see that there's a long
line of people in front of the counter. *Blah!* Who's got the
time to be standing here for hours on end? I wonder how
much time has been wasted standing in this line, among the
stacks of lame greeting cards and junky pen and pencil sets?

But then I see Tenzin Choepel. I haven't seen him since
yesterday, when he asked me to the dance and I ran away.
I'm sure he thinks I'm a rude, ungrateful weirdo, but he
waves and makes a space in front of him and I slip into the
line.

"It looks like you have some special letters to post," Tenzin smiles, and I can tell he's forgiven me.

I explain that it's my Nan's seventieth birthday coming up and I've got 35 stamps to buy and lick and stick. I'm not sure how long that will take. For-ev-er, by the looks of things.

"You're lucky to have your grandmother living near you," says Tenzin. "All four of my grandparents are still back in Tibet. But we write every week," he says, waving a fat letter in my face. "All of us, my mother and father and two sisters, sit down every Sunday and write a page each. And we send cards and photographs. Although we have to write the addresses in the Chinese language – not in Tibetan – or they won't be delivered. We are very much hoping that they can come and live here with us in Britannia one day."

I ask Tenzin if he ever calls his grandparents.

"Oh, they've never had a telephone," he laughs. "And we can't ring any of our other relatives because just one phone call could mean serious trouble for them. Our letters are carried to our grandparents' village in the mountains on the back of a yak."

Hah! Yak mail? That's awesome! Sure beats my dad driving his van around Oldcastle for Ascot Couriers. I ask Tenzin if they've had to sack any yaks because of the GFC *and everything.*

Tenzin giggles and his laugh reminds me of the ringing brass finger cymbals he played for us in last year's school concert. He wore a traditional embroidered costume and

played while his sisters performed a Tibetan folk dance. I
remember Carmelita nudging me and telling me how cute
he was. He has incredibly white teeth and sparkling dark
brown eyes set in a face the color of sugar toffee.

"I'm going to ask you something, and I hope you don't
run off this time," he grins.

I duck my head; the memory of that moment is still
excruciating.

"Would you like to come with me to the Tibetan
Freedom Festival next Sunday? The Buddhist monks are
making a sand mandala in the name of peace at the Gummy
Beach Surf Club."

I look at him blankly.

"A sand mandala is a healing circle. The monks have
been there all week making a beautiful picture by pouring
colored sand onto a table. There are representations of
deities, monkeys, victory banners and patterns of the five
elements – wood, fire, earth, water and metal.

"On Sunday morning they'll have a special ceremony
and gather all the sand in jars. They'll make a procession
across the beach and say prayers as they tip all the sand into
the water."

I can't believe all that work just gets dumped into the
ocean. Why?

"To symbolize the cycle of life and the impermanence of
existence." Tenzin holds up his letter and smiles. "We write
letters and take photographs to remind everyone who we

are, and what we are thinking, but one day everything will be swept away."

It all sounds so amazing. I find myself telling Tenzin that I would very much like to go with him to see the ceremony.

"That's great. So I'll ring you," he says.

I explain that it might be difficult to get in touch because I don't have a telephone ... or a computer.

"Then I shall send a yak!" Tenzin declares.

And we are both laughing so hard that the old lady in front of us turns and gives us an evil stare.

Soon enough I'm at the counter and I pay up for a sheet of stamps with Russell Crowe's face on them. I wasn't looking forward to licking the back of his head, but these ones are self-adhesive.

It's all a lot easier than I thought it would be and there's something so satisfying about lifting the lid on the metal mailbox and hearing the envelopes flutter into the heap below. I can't quite believe there are so many letters still migrating around the globe. I wish my envelopes *bon voyage* and let the lid go. It shuts with a *clang!*

Tenzin and I stroll together to the end of Kensington Street and exchange addresses.

"And the dance on Saturday? Do you have a date?" he asks.

I tell him that Carmelita's coming down from Queensland and that we've decided to go together.

"My mother wants me to take my younger sister, so I'll

be free to have a dance with both of you," he grins.

I nod, that will be great. Then Tenzin walks away with a long and easy stride – head up, facing the afternoon sun. There's something about that boy I like very much.

I head back along the other side of the street, thinking about what Tenzin says about the impermanence of life. All the photographs I had on my computer were like a sand mandala. Gathered over ten months and swept away in a moment.

I wonder how long I'll remember all the great times Will and I had together if I can't look back at the photographs of us hanging at the skate park or in his front yard at Hammerhead. When I'm as old as Nan, will I be able to remember the tiny globs of salt in his hair and the minuscule drops of water on his eyelashes? I won't even have a crumbling bunch of roses to remind me of my boy.

I should start making my own box of memories to treasure. Something I could take with me if I ever had to leave my home and cross a river in the dead of night. My christening bracelet and necklace and a couple of baby teeth are in my ballerina music box. I know Mum's got my old school reports and some of my first bits of arts and crafts packed away somewhere. I had lots of things stored on my hard drive that maybe should have been saved and stored in a box, or at the very least in my head.

I've stopped in my tracks thinking about all this and when I look up I find myself outside the narrow shop window of Royal Seal Stationery. When I step inside I see it's absolutely crammed with divine writing paper, envelopes, stamps, inks, pens, cards and ribbons. I adore every single thing and spend ages poking through all the shelves.

In the end I choose some thick notepaper decorated in the left-hand corner with a tangerine tree and a bluebird sitting in the branches. It's in a lovely box, with matching envelopes, tied with striped orange ribbon. I also choose a white fountain pen and a bottle of Jewel Green Old English writing ink.

Then I head home to finish making the curry puffs for dinner.

Tuesday. 8 p.m.
PM. AW. PPC.

I've written one letter to Carmelita and one to my cousin
Anne in Toolewong. They should both get a surprise
when they open their mailboxes and see the pale orange
envelope decorated with tangerines and bluebirds and
addressed in green ink!

I wonder what my handwriting says about me? Then
I decide to write Nan a note too and I'll ask her what she
thinks when I'm over there next Sunday.

Mum enters The Dungeon and leans over my shoulder.

"You're writing letters with a fountain pen? Good for you,
Elly," she exclaims. "Truly, I never thought I'd see the day!"

"I used to have pen pals when I was your age." Mum
chuckles at the memory and sits on the bed. "I remember

buying teenage magazines and there would always be this page headed 'pen pals wanted.' I wrote for years to a boy in Brussels and a girl in Hong Kong!

"Oooh, he was gorgeous, that boy. He used to sign himself 'Your Romeo of Belgium' and I used to go all silly over his letters. He once sent me a photograph of himself standing in the snow in a full-length fur coat and I used to think he was the handsomest bloke in the world – a bit like Steve Tyler."

Who?

"Steve Tyler from Aerosmith. Oh, I adored him – those tight pants and high-heeled boots, his wild hair and big pouting lips. I remember their slogan: We're the band your mother warned you about. And Mum did hit the roof whenever I played their albums."

Why does Mum always seem to wander off down memory lane when she sits on my bed? This Steve Tyler person is still not ringing any bells.

"He's Liv Tyler's father," Mum explains. "Wasn't she Arwen Evenstar in Lord of the Rings?"

Oh, that's right, I remember now that Liv's got a famous rock star father. An image of Will as an elf enters my mind and I shake my head to make it go away.

"You know, I think I've still got some of my pen pal letters somewhere." Mum leaps off the bed and runs down the hallway.

I can hear her rummaging in the linen closet and when

I look out she's almost up to her neck in busted tennis racquets, moldy ski gear and flippers.

"Here! Here they are," she says, triumphantly holding up a battered shoebox.

We spend the next hour going through her mementos: her ID card from the Britannia Institute of Technology, her first driver's license, concert tickets, cards from Dad and all her letters. There's even some of her old poetry in here that's been typed on sheets of paper and is covered with patches of flaking white ink sort of gunk.

Yikes! Most of the poetry is about her walking along the beach *under the moon, in June* and it really, absolutely, sucks. There's a lot of stuff from up until she was about the same age as Tilly, then there's nothing much after that.

"I probably stopped putting things in this box about the time Margie and I got our first personal computer. Your pop brought home this huge, clunky thing. But we loved it and it meant we could get rid of the old typewriter and ribbons and bottles of White Out that always used to spill on the desk. I suppose there's a computer somewhere down at the dump with all my Britannia Institute work on it."

Mum packs everything away and she's singing *walk this way, talk this way* … whatever that means. She says it's an Aerosmith song. (Yikes!) I truly never knew she had this box. Amazing to think it's gone undiscovered after all the years Tilly and I have searched every square inch of the house looking for hidden birthday and Christmas presents.

193

"Do you know," says Mum, as she looks again at the letter I am writing to Nan, "your handwriting is quite lovely, Els. I think you just might have a talent for calligraphy. At the moment I have to pay someone to do all the table place cards and invitations for weddings and parties ... but if you could do them? That'd be really something, wouldn't it?"

It would! It's a brilliant idea! I've seen lots of the cards Mum gets done in calligraphy and I've always loved the gorgeous script in black ink – all the lovely loops and flourishes. I must admit I've never thought of trying to learn how to do it myself.

Mum fishes in the back pocket of her jeans and produces thirty dollars.

"Here, take this and when you're next down the street buy yourself some pens, paper and more ink," says Mum. "While you don't have a computer you might as well take up a hobby."

A *hobby*? Aren't hobbies for really pathetic people who've got all the time in the world and nothing to do? And then I realize that without any technology, a boyfriend, or a BF in town, I'm *exactly* the person who should have a hobby.

Wednesday. 7:30 p.m.
PM. AW. PPC.

"What are you doing?" says Tilly, as she stands behind me and looks at the pile of scrunched-up notepaper, bottles of ink and scattered pen nibs where my computer used to be.

How kind of you to visit!

I'm looking at my black, ink-stained fingers and wondering the same. This is a lot harder than it looks. I went back to the Royal Seal and bought a calligraphy set with everything I need. I've now read that the history of calligraphy goes back thousands of years and that people can take a lifetime to become a "Scribe Master." Sadly my attempts at a lower-case "a" in Chancery font look like a squashed funnel-web spider.

"Calligraphy?" Tilly shakes her head in disbelief.

"Honestly, you need a new computer. You can choose from zillions of fonts on there. Next thing you'll be sticking ballet trading cards in an album."

I snort. Surely no one was ever that weird.

Tilly grimaces back. "Pretty sad, huh?"

She looks paler than usual tonight and has dark rings under her eyes. Her first exam is next Monday. I'm really not looking forward to doing the HSC exams. All the Year Twelves at school are walking around like zombies.

"Better get back to it," Tilly says wearily. "I've got Eddie's laptop here and I just have to figure out how to get on to the Net from my room. I've still got the modem and wireless, so it should be OK." She stops at the door and looks at me awkwardly. "And, uh, I just wanted to tell you that Jayden and Lily are back together."

I know that already. Unlike Tilly, I haven't been living under a rock.

"I'm trying to find out from Georgie Daniels what went down. Who dumped who and all that, but a lot of people are off this week on study leave and keeping weird hours, so it's been kinda hard."

I stare at the bare corkboard in front of me and tell Tilly that I don't care and I really should put some shots of ... something ... in the empty space where Will used to be.

"Good. Move on. That's best," she says. She's distracted and doesn't notice that I'm lying through my teeth, because I *do* care. "I'll see you later." She sighs noisily and plods off to the South Wing.

Do please come again!

I haven't moved on. Not yet. I miss Will so much. I'd love to write him a letter, but I don't know what I'd say. In about a thousand years when I'm a Scribe Master, I might have just about worked it out.

Yours most sincerely, Miss E. E. Pickering.

Thursday. 10:30 a.m.
PM. AW. PPC.

It's torture time in Drama with Fergie again.

"How many of you people have visited the library so far?" she squawks.

I look around and see that quite a few people have their hands up. I accidentally look Bianca in the eye and she makes this sad face at me and I almost laugh. This morning she's got two straggly bunches of ratty hair hanging on either side of her face and she looks like an Afghan hound! I'm pleased to see that without my supervision her hair's going from bad to *Woof!*

I'll never forgive her for saying that I was dumped by Will because no one likes me. I haven't spoken to her for two whole days and I suspect she is spreading stories about me – in person and by every available known technology.

It certainly feels like everyone's avoiding me at the moment. Without Bianca and Carmelita I don't really have that many close girlfriends here at Oldcastle. I guess I relied on being with Bianca and Carmelita for years and I didn't bother to make new friends. I stare back at Bianca until she turns away and starts gossiping behind her hand to that total airhead Rosie Di Masi who's sitting next to her. Then Bianca and Rosie both look sideways at me, point their fingers and start smirking.

Fergie *harrumphs* and stomps her feet for attention. I can see her temperature rise until all her freckles stand out like brown pebbles on Wobbegong Beach.

"Bianca Ponsford! I'm looking at YOU! Although I can hardly see your face under all that silly hair. Have you been to the library yet?"

"No, Mrs. Ferguson."

"Then I will be expecting you to GET ON WITH IT!" Fergie yells from the front of the room. "I want those assignments in by Monday!"

I'm looking beyond the classroom to the beautiful spring day outside when I see Will's blond curls bob by the window. I make an instant decision to spend this lunchtime inside the library. For once, maybe old bat Fergie's had a good idea.

✳

I'm sitting in the library in a sunny spot by the window. I

figure that if Fergie's ordered Bianca to come here, then it's the last place she'll be. I'm up to the bit in *Jane Eyre* where Jane has first gone to Lowood School and has no friends.

Those poor wretched girls endured coarse straw bonnets, scratchy woolen dresses, freezing cold beds, frozen pitchers of water, no heating, not enough blankets, burnt porridge, thin slices of brown bread and scrapes of butter – it makes my heart ache to read about it. I'll never complain again when they forget the cheese on my ham and cheese roll at the school shop!

Now I've just read chapters seven and eight where Jane Eyre's humiliated by the hideous Mr. Brocklehurst for breaking her slate (i.e. she loses her mobile at the mall). It's the quiet and gentle Helen Burns who, in the middle of all this hideousness, has the humanity and generosity of spirit to come and comfort Jane.

> *Hush, Jane! you think too much of the love of human beings; you are too impulsive, too vehement: the sovereign hand that created your frame, and put life into it, has provided you with other resources than your feeble self, or than creatures feeble as you.*

It's another way of saying what I already know – that I shouldn't care so much what other people think of me – or don't think of me. It's what Carmelita always says. (Although if Carmelita had been at Lowood, she would have had everyone dancing on the tables, using chunks of brown bread as maracas and chucking burnt porridge at that slimy toad Brocklehurst.)

Now that I'm not checking FacePlace or my phone every five minutes, I'm starting to see all this stuff around me that I never noticed before. There are more resources to call on other than my *feeble self.*

Sun Tzu, sand mandalas, Scrabble, stationery, love letters, calligraphy and now *Jane Eyre*. It's all crazy stuff I'd never have really thought about if I was still sitting with Bianca at the mall spotting fashion crimes.

I remember what I thought when my handbag first went missing with my mobile and my friendship ring: *I wonder if things go missing for a reason. As if by their absence, they might be trying to tell you something. To make you see life in a new way.*

In the library stacks there are heaps of books about the Brontë sisters. I read a bit here and there, photocopy some pages, write my bibliography and my assignment is done and dusted. That should get that bag Fergie off my back.

My thanks are due to those who have inclined an indulgent ear to a plain tale with few pretensions.

Friday. 6 p.m.
PM. AW. PPC.

CARMELITA! CARMELITA! *Carmelita!*

I'm singing her name in a flamenco rhythm and she's dancing wildly to it at the Palace gate, tapping her feet and waving her arms in the air. Her gorgeous black curls are whirling around her face. I can't believe she's here!

"OHHHH! AAARGH! ELLY! ELLY!" She drops her bag and runs down our driveway screeching like a crazy Spanish chicken. "I've missed you so, so much! And thank you for the letter. Those bluebirds were the most gorgeous things ever!"

In a moment Carmelita's in my arms and I am snuffling and crying into her hair. It's like every bit of emotion from the past two weeks has rolled into one big, steaming … paella.

Soon enough we're in The Dungeon and I'm watching her reacquainting herself with her vast collection of pigs. She's cooing over every one with motherly affection. It's an incredibly cute reunion. She's brought me a present: a pig candle. It's scented with mandarin and bergamot.

Once Carmelita's propped up on my bed, cradling my pink stuffed pig, and I've extravagantly admired her black lace-up boots, paisley skirt, little black jacket, silver locket and, *sigh!,* everything about her – and then she's complimented me on my new white peasant top and jeweled flip-flops – it's time to get down to business. There's so much to talk about and I'm not sure where to start.

"I've got a boyfriend," Carmelita blurts.

Ooh, this is BIG news. Carmelita's never had time for boys. She's always been too busy laughing at them to take them seriously.

"He lives on the pineapple farm up the road, his name's Henry and he's D.I.V.I.N.E. – divine!" she gives the pig a smothering smooch. "Here's a snap of His Loveliness," she says, and hands over her mobile.

I'm looking at a face smattered with freckles, a pair of bright blue eyes with fair eyelashes and a haystack of ginger hair. His smile's so wide you'd think he'd swallowed a banana.

"We've been seeing each other for about a month. He comes over to our farm on his motorbike to help me with Viscount. He brings me pineapples and, Els, that's so appropriate because he really is the sweetest, sunniest thing in the universe."

Carmelita's dark eyes are shining with happiness and I'm thrilled for her.

"And Els, you want to know something?"

I do. I want to know everything!

"We were down at the back paddock with the tractor on Wednesday night, by the river watching the sunset, and he told me ..."

Carmelita pauses here for dramatic effect and I know what's coming.

"... *that he loved me!*"

This is the best news and in an instant I'm jumping on the bed with Carmelita – even as one self-obsessed part of my brain is remembering that in ten whole months Will never told me that he loved me.

After I've heard every necessary detail about this Henry – even down to the fact that, tragically, he's allergic to macadamia nuts – it's time to get around to the multi-car pileup that is my life.

Carmelita notices that there are no pictures of Will on my wall.

"Have you talked to him yet?" she asks.

No. It's been a week now since that night he was at Lily Cameron's place, and we haven't spoken since that Saturday morning on Winchester Headland.

"You know you're going to have to," she says, taking my shoulders in her hands and giving them a shake, her eyes drilling into mine. "You can't just throw ten whole months of your life on the scrapheap without any explanation."

I tell her what Bianca said – that I wasn't cool or popular enough for Will.

"Ha ha ha, that's hilarious!" Carmelita throws the stuffed pig at my head. "'Cos, of course Ponsford is an expert in human relationships and everyone at Oldcastle is just *drooling* over Jai the Jerk!"

I duck my head. What can I say? *I'm a stupid idiot!*

"Bianca is utterly brainless. You can see right through her head – in one ear and out the other! I can't believe you'd take her word for anything. If she said it was raining you'd have to open the window to see for sure. You have to speak to Will *himself*. Has he tried to call or come over or email or anything?"

I tell Carmelita that he came to visit, but Dad sent him away, and there was that eye2eye that Tilly deleted.

"And why do you think he'd bother to contact you if he wanted to be with Lily Cameron?"

I tell her that I really don't know. And, BTW, they're not together anymore.

"If they ever *were*," Carmelita says with a shrug.

But the photos ...

"Hah! There are still people around who reckon NASA

faked the moon landing. Never take anything at face value, Els. Ya gotta find out for yourself. And if you're too pathetic to see Will, then I'm going to."

Don't bother, I sniff. Will never loved me, so maybe he's happier without me.

"Yeah, right! The only time Will Phillips ever says he's in love is when he's got a new surfboard. He's never going to admit that he loves a *girl!*"

Well then, maybe he's not the sort of boy I want to be with.

"That could be true. That could well be true. And it's something you have to think about. But you'll never know what sort of boy you *want* unless you know what sort of boy you *had*. Am I right?"

Carmelita's always right. And that's why I love her so.

"OK, that's sorted. Now let's get on to the all-important topic of what you're going to wear to the dance tomorrow night. What do you think of this?"

Carmelita drags a red ruffled crepe three-quarter-length dress from her bag, holds it up against herself and twirls for me. I give her a standing ovation. It's perfect. Just perfect. With her black curls and olive skin she looks like a gypsy princess. A pair of red patent leather stilettos complete the picture.

"And what about you, Els? What are you wearing? Lemme see."

I explain that my outfit is, at this moment, probably

scrunched into a little ball at the bottom of the Tilly closet.

It's about time we made a strategic raid on her room.

After about an hour of sifting through the pile of clothes like a couple of fevered prospectors, I strike gold – a shimmering minidress with fab long, flowing sleeves and a low scooped back. I try it on.

"Oh Els, you look as yummy as a Ferrero Rocher in all that gold," swoons Carmelita. "Sweet."

My heart lurches when I remember that's what Will always says. "Sweet." I wonder if he'll be at the dance tomorrow night? What will I say if I bump into him?

There's one thing I do know – and that's that I am going to look as stunning as I possibly can to show Will what he's missing! Carmelita and I continue our mining expedition looking for Tilly's exquisite new silver strappy high-heeled sandals. I find them and Carmelita squeals her approval.

"They are To. Die. For! You're so lucky having a big sister," she sighs.

Sometimes I'm not sure about that, but I know that I'm lucky Tilly's studying, which means I should be able to get this stuff back under the pile before she notices I've borrowed it.

A little silver sequined shoulder bag is added to my booty and we sneak back to The Dungeon with my stolen treasures.

Carmelita flops on the bed and starts unlacing her boots.

"OK, babe! It's time for pedicures! *La cu-ca-ra-cha!*"

And with two mighty *thuds*, Carmelita's boots hit the wall.

Saturday. 4 p.m.
PM. AW. PPC.

I'm standing inside the doors of St. John's Church, West Oldcastle, helping my mum hand out wedding programs and asking the same question over and over: *Are you with the bride or with the groom?*

Who cares? After all, I'm assuming that everyone will be one big happy family after this joyous occasion.

As much as I hate to say it, I wish Bianca Ponsford was here. It's a sad waste to be in Fashion Crime Central on my own. I've racked up at least five positively identified style transgressions in this congregation without even trying.

1. White lace stockings with sling-backs – No! No! No!

2. Purple silk puffball skirt – You look like a poisonous toadstool, madam.

3. Embroidered suit lapels with shoestring tie – more Riverboat Gambler than Father of the Bride.

4. Sequins, silk flowers, bugle beads *and* ribbons – Enough decoration for a bridal party of ten, all herded onto *one* individual.

5. Red feather fascinator. *Here, chickie, chickie, chickie!*

Bianca would be in a frenzy by now. Her head would have swiveled so many times that it probably would've unscrewed right off the top of her neck and fallen in the font.

Still, I've earned $20 since I got here. By the end of the day – putting together all the $$$ I have collected through folding paper napkins into the shape of swans and tying paper scrolls with red ribbons – I think I will almost have enough for a new mobile! YAAAY!

When the bride arrives right on cue (AKA twenty minutes late) I am about to expire of boredom. So there's no one more surprised than me when I get a lump in my throat as the bridal party finally assembles at the top of the aisle.

Of course, I'd rather kill myself than wear a burgundy taffeta bridesmaid's dress. I'd rather stick pins in my eyes than carry a cane basket full of white daisies. And the wedding dress looks like a pavlova topped with fruit salad. But when I see that the bride is so nervous and weepy on her big day, I can't help feeling a bit like crying myself. (Although that *could* be because her face is framed with ghastly tendrils of hair that make her look as if she's being attacked by a couple of brown snakes.)

But no, by the time the bride is halfway down the aisle to the strains of Mrs. Winchester (my old kindergarten teacher from Oldcastle Primary), belting out "Ave Maria" from the organ loft, I'm a wreck. I guess it's only to be expected. Everything makes me cry lately.

As the bride and groom make their vows, I'm searching for a packet of tissues in my awful old leather bag. (*Where art thou*, my lost and beautiful butter-yellow handbag?) I step outside into the vestry where I figure I can have a good old honk and not interrupt the congregation.

And then the tears flow. I'm thinking about Will and how much I miss seeing him and talking to him. It's like I'm being pelted with stinging grains of rice.

While my head is bent – so no one can see me howling like a stupid idiot – I suddenly hear a rapid *crunch, crunch, crunch* on crushed white quartz. I look up and see ... *Carmelita?* She's supposed to be at her Auntie Isabella's birthday party. She's waving her arms in the air and doing that mental Spanish poultry thing again. Skipping up the driveway like a crazy hen.

"ELLY! I went to see Will! I found out what happened!"

she shouts.

I tell her to *shoosh* – Mum is lurking somewhere within hearing distance.

Carmelita rushes up and takes me in her arms and lifts me off the ground and spins me around. She sweeps my long hair from one shoulder with red fingernails and her breath is hot in my ear.

"It was the ring, the ring, *the ring*!"

What *ring*? The ring of my mobile, church bells … Frodo's ring?

"Will was calling and texting Lily and eventually went to see her because he wanted to replace the ring you lost!" Carmelita babbles.

Is she talking about my silver ring with the tiny blue stones? It was so precious. Now forever lost down a crevice in the Mount Doom mall.

"He wanted to show you how much he loved you by getting her to hand-make another ring. 'Specially for you. She makes jewelry, right? He wanted you to know that there would never, ever be another like yours on the face of the earth."

I suddenly realize that what I saw under the jacaranda tree made sense. That envelope Lily held out to Will? Was my ring inside it?

"And the photos of him and Lily," Carmelita's still gabbling in my face. "He says she pushed him into getting in the spa and it was all just innocent stuff. So he thought.

Then when he realized Lily was coming on to him, he insisted they get out and he left. He never dreamed someone was taking photos and they would end up on FacePlace."

But I saw the photos ... everyone saw.

"But they didn't *mean* anything. It was all just a mistake. He loves you so much, Elly! He loves you with all his heart. I swear. On the heart of Viscount the Pig, I swear." Carmelita stands back, looks to the heavens and solemnly makes the sign of the cross.

"Would you two just *SHOOSH!*" says my mum, as she charges out the door flapping a wedding program at us. "They're about to exchange rings and all we can hear in there is a couple of bird brains gossiping –" Mum looks up to the church spire – "like a pair of silly pigeons."

Mum's made a mistake. There are no pigeons on the spire of St. John's Church this afternoon. Instead I see two white doves taking to the dusky sky.

They take my heart with them.

Saturday. 6 p.m.
PM. AW. PPC.

I get back to the Palace to frock up for the dance. Carmelita's getting changed at her Auntie Isabella's place and I'm going to meet her at Lord's boathouse on the south bank of the Mersey River.

As I walk up the hall there's a light coming from under the door in the South Wing and I know Tilly will be hitting the books. When I open the door I can see she's sitting hunched over her desk, which is piled high with dirty coffee cups and plates. She's almost up to her knees in clothes and looks like one of those poor kids you see in destitute countries who have to live on trash dumps.

"Oh hey, Elly," she whispers. "Come on in – if you can find a place to sit."

She waves at where the bed is supposed to be, although under the leaning towers of junk it's hard to tell. When I land with a bounce and grin at her, she squints at me through the gloom.

"Hmmm, you're looking happier than I've seen you for a while."

I tell her everything that Carmelita told me. That it was all just a big mistake, that the reason Will was calling Lily was to get her to make me a new friendship ring!

"That's what I heard too. Georgie told me this afternoon. Lily used Will to make Jayden jealous. And it worked on that dribbling idiot. Honestly, can you believe a sweet girl who makes such pretty jewelry could be such a ..."

Words fail Tilly here as she holds her arm up to the light and jangles the delicate bracelet Lily made. I don't care. I don't want to spoil my mood with complaining about Lily Cameron. Everyone makes massive mistakes when they're heartbroken.

"If I'd stayed and spoken to Will that night, none of this would have happened," Tilly says. "So I'm sorry for that, Els, and I'm sorry I talked you into paying out on him on FacePlace too."

I tell her it's OK. I should have taken notice of the warning that emotions and the Internet don't mix. And if I hadn't been guilty of the five dangerous sins a general can make, I wouldn't even have been in a war in the first place.

I lean across Tilly and Google *The Art of War* on Eddie's

215

laptop. There it is – the best leaders conquer the enemy before they enter battle. They win by using strategy.

And the best strategy would have been to go to see Jai, explain that he'd hurt my feelings and ask him to please take down those embarrassing photographs from FacePlace.

"Who's Sun Tzu?" Tilly looks nonplussed. "What *are* you on about? What with this babble, and your calligraphy, little sister, you're becoming more inscrutable by the day."

I smile at this. *Inscrutable*. It's good. I like it. It's way more interesting than telling everyone everything about you every minute of the day.

"I closed my FacePlace site this afternoon," says Tilly, as she leans back and stretches. "I'm over all the gossipy stuff that goes on there. You always find that the people who post most are the ones that have got the least to say."

I think of Bianca's incessant mirror scribblings and the hundreds of photos she posts and I know that it's true.

"So what happens now? Do you want to borrow my mobile and call Will?" asks Tilly.

I shake my head. I have to think this through. I'll see him tonight, I suppose. Don't know what I'll say. And maybe he won't say anything and I'll have to try to read his mind – as usual.

Is that the kind of boy I really want, I wonder aloud. Do I want a boy at all?

"Atta girl! Now you're starting to wise up. You're amazing, Eleanor. I love you, I really do," Tilly declares.

Then she springs from her chair in a flying leap and pins me on the bed with her bony knees. AAARGH! I wrestle back and flip her on her tummy and then mash her face into the pillows.

"OW, OW, OW!" she screeches. "Get off! I've got a lip balm in my eye!"

There's a *thump thump thump* on the wall.

"OI! KEEP IT DOWN IN THERE, YOU TWO," Dad bellows through the wall from the throne room.

And we two Royal Princesses from Buckingham Palace, Oldcastle, laugh our tiaras off.

Saturday. 7 p.m.
PM. AW. PCC.

"*Ma belle*, you'll be the most gorgeous thing at the dance tonight," says Dad, as he reaches for his jacket.

"Look at you, just look at you!" exclaims Mum, clapping her hands, and for once she's not talking about the dog. "Rick, get the camera."

I pose this way and that, totally enjoying my star turn in front of the paparazzi in the Palace kitchen.

Tilly appears in the doorway in her dressing gown with her empty coffee cup and her mouth drops open. "Hey! Isn't that my ...?"

I'm stuttering some sort of lame apology when she just shakes her head.

"Go for it. You look amazing. I love your hair up like

that, but I hate it when you look better in my clothes than I do. I *so* forgot I even had that dress."

"No wonder, with the state of that pigsty you live in." Mum *has* to take the opportunity to get a nag in.

"Hey, Mum," sings Tilly, as she reaches for the kettle. "One day Elly and I won't be living here and you'll be standing in our empty rooms and missing our stinky, girly stuff."

Tilly and I both start to laugh and then I see Mum's face crumple.

"Don't," she blubs into her hands. "Don't. I can't stand the thought of it."

Dad throws his arm around Mum and gives her a hug.

"Don't worry, darls! When the girls move out, we'll sell this place and I'll take you on a trip to see the real Buckingham Palace! So, Elly, let's get going. Your coach awaits!"

Mum brightens up a bit and the Royal Family of Oldcastle all have a soppy group hug.

Then I'm flying out the door on silver sandals. Princess Elly, on her way to the ball! Suddenly there's a strangled screech from behind me.

"NO, NO ELLY! NOT MY NEW SHOES. YOU CAN'T WEAR THEM!"

Too late! I sprint down the path and lock the car door behind me. Tilly owes me these shoes. She's standing on the front porch, still giving me the stare of death, as Dad backs the car down the driveway.

Saturday. 8 p.m.
PM. AW. PCC.

Actually, it's more like a little kid's birthday party than a fairytale ball here at the boathouse tonight. Paper streamers and balloons are sagging from the ceiling. Streamers? Balloons? Then again, maybe they do suit the place – some of the Year Eights tottering around on their high heels look about eight years old.

I wouldn't be surprised to see them with goody bags at the end of the night. It's all a bit pathetic. Why do we have to share our dance with the grommets? Why can't they have a bouncy castle in the school courtyard?

The Year Elevens and Twelves all get to dress in long gowns and tuxedos and dance to a live band at their formal in November. Meanwhile, over in a dingy corner I see that ridiculous dropkick Bad Mickey B standing under a CASTLEROCK 64.5 FM banner playing DJ and thinking he's the King of the World. Standing next to him is the hideous Jai, punching the air with his fists and imagining he's in some special VIP area. It's truly, truly sad.

I'm just wondering whether Will will even make it here tonight when Carmelita catches me by the elbow and spins me around. We both give each other total five stars. Carmelita has never, ever looked prettier. She's a totally hot red carpet babe!

We walk arm-in-arm to the outside deck and I have to admit that with the lights of Britannia reflected in the still waters of the Mersey, there might be a touch of magic about the evening. And what of Prince Charming? Again the thought of seeing him makes my stomach flip.

"CARMELITA! What are YOU doing here?" shrieks Bianca from behind us. "Did you bring your pig? Where are your gumboots?"

Oh, v.v. funny!

I turn to see Bianca's hair so puffed up and teased and sprayed that it might double for a shipping hazard buoy on the Mersey River. What *has* she done to herself?

"Hi Bianca! *Love* your hair!" says Carmelita, as she gives me a secret kick in the shins.

"Me too," I chirp, trying not to laugh.

"I'm just back in Oldcastle for the weekend and I thought I'd be Elly's date," says Carmelita.

"Well, why not?" Bianca sneers. "Doesn't look like any of the seaweed heads you usually hang with are here tonight, Elly."

I just smile. I'm practicing being inscrutable. I know it will drive Bianca crazy.

And then "Get the Party Started" by Pink thumps through the speakers inside and we push past Bianca and hit the polished wooden dance floor, determined to show the tinys from Year Eight how it's done.

We prance on our high heels under the tacky disco lights and ... it feels so brilliant to be dancing! Not thinking anything at all. Just dancing. Kicking up my exquisite heels with my BFF Carmelita.

"Did you smell Bianca's breath?" Carmelita leans and yells into my ear over the music. "I think she's been drinking alcohol."

No! I make an astonished face at Carmelita. I am just about to try and get more information when Tenzin rocks up.

"I am here to dance with both of you!" he shouts. "The two prettiest girls in Oldcastle. This is my lucky night!"

Saturday. 9 p.m.
PM. AW. PCC.

There's still no sign of Will and I'm sort of glad in a way, because Carmelita and I can't take our eyes off Bianca. She's standing with Jai and Bad Mickey B behind the DJ's table and during the past hour we have both spotted her drinking what's supposed to be non-alcoholic punch, but we reckon it's something she's getting from a suspicious thermos stashed behind the speaker stack.

There's a break in the music and a stampede for the supper table.

It's like a watering hole in Africa. Sir David Attenborough would love to narrate this scene for the National Geographic Channel. He'd note how the Year Eights all herd at one end of the table to feed, the Year Nines at the other end, and how the Year Tens all stand back while they let the animals lower down the food chain have their fill before they amble over to graze.

Carmelita and I load our paper plates with vegetarian pizza and little tomato and cheese tartlets and find ourselves a quiet corner.

Carmelita nudges me and I look up from my plate to see the apparition of Fergie coming towards us in full flight.

Uh-oh!

She's marching across the dance floor towards us in the ugliest sack-like floral dress and white platforms that have ever been seen in Oldcastle – which is really saying something! Tonight she's wearing her *formal* scrunchie – black polyester with gold beads sewn on it.

"Elly Pickering. Carmelita Martinez," she says officiously. "A quiet word."

I gulp. Usually Fergie's yelling at full volume. This must be seriously serious.

"Bianca Ponsford is ... er ... unwell," says Fergie, in a hoarse whisper.

"That's because she's been drinking alcohol," says Carmelita, who's not known for being the most tactful person on earth. "We saw her filling her glass from a thermos."

"Well, yes. Quite right," says Fergie, looking around and hoping no one's overheard. "The drink was brought into the venue by Jai McHaargh and he has already been picked up by his parents."

Carmelita and I exchange a look. It's exactly what we suspected. And Jai's already gone home? Funny, no one seems to have missed him.

"I would like you two girls, as Bianca's best friends, to see her outside and put her into a taxi. I've ordered the car and it should be out front in five minutes."

Huh! I look at Carmelita. Why us? Why do we have to be Bianca's minders?

"We are short-staffed tonight," Fergie explains. "Myself, Mr. York and Mr. Battenburg cannot leave the other one hundred and fifty pupils here unsupervised – one of those silly Year Eights could jump off the deck and drown in the river in an instant – so I am asking you to please, please lend a hand."

"Can't her mum and dad come and get her?" asks Carmelita through a mouthful of pizza. We've been dancing nonstop in heels and we both need to sit down and rest our throbbing feet.

Fergie looks utterly stressed out and I actually feel a bit sorry for her.

"I've rung Bianca's parents and unfortunately they've been drinking as well and are unable to drive. They are expecting her home shortly. Of course, as soon as you see her off, you can come back and join the celebrations. Bianca's waiting by the front door now, so please go quickly and quietly. I am counting on your utmost discretion."

Looks like we've got no option. We grab our handbags

and trudge towards the front door. Bianca Ponsford! What a total pain!

At the front door of the boathouse we see Bianca leaning against a tall wooden oar, trying to keep herself upright. Her inflatable hairdo is slowly collapsing into an ugly mess.

"Smelly! Camel!" Bianca turns and waves, dropping her mobile on the floor with a nasty clatter. The back springs off, and skids across the tiles. The battery rolls under a cupboard. Bianca falls to her knees with a bruising *thud* as she gropes for the bits.

Carmelita finds everything and puts the precious device back together. Then we each take one of Bianca's upper arms, haul her to her feet and steer her out into the street.

"Thank youse. I love youse," she slurs.

The three of us are standing in the freezing night air waiting for the stupid taxi when I see Will walk up with Bombie Logan! Will is so surprised to see me that he trips on the curb.

"HA!" shouts Bianca. "Flipper feet!"

Which is pretty ironic coming from Bianca, who, without me and Carmelita holding her up, would fall flat on her face and be swept down the street into the river.

"Hey! Will, Bombie!" calls Carmelita.

"Yo! Carmelita!" Bombie ambles over and surveys the scene. He looks at Bianca with disgust. Honestly, if she saw what a disgrace her makeup looks, she would never drink again. Her lipstick is smeared halfway down her chin and her smudged mascara makes her face look like a Halloween mask.

"What's happening?" asks Bombie. I notice Will's hanging back in the shadows.

"We've got a slight situation here," Carmelita explains. "We're just waiting for a taxi to take Bianca home and we'll be back inside in a couple of minutes. Save us a dance?"

I dare to look up at Will and I can almost feel my legs give way too. It's my Will. He's as beautiful tonight as he ever has been.

"Uh, sure," says Will, staring down at the ground. "See you inside in a minute, then."

"Cool," says Bombie, and they both shove their hands even deeper into their pockets and shuffle past us. Will's so close to me. My old life is so near to me I could reach out and touch it. There's only one thing between me and true happiness – Bianca Pontoon Head Ponsford!

GRRRRR! Ten minutes have gone by now and the taxi still hasn't come. Forget a foil-wrapped chocolate, I'm turning into an ice cream bar! Carmelita's stamping her red stilettos, trying to keep warm.

"WHERE'S THAT STUPID TAXI?" she wails.

Bianca's been trying to call someone on her mobile the whole time. She's been randomly stabbing at the keypad and I wouldn't be surprised if she's managed to ring Tenzin's family in Tibet and their house is surrounded by Chinese soldiers by now.

Then Bianca is startled by a *ping* on her mobile and she reads the message.

"NOOOOOOO!" she moans. She stumbles forward, executes a startling 360-degree turn and falls dramatically backwards into my arms. Weeping blue eyes ringed with black and purple sludge stare up at me.

"It's Jai!" she sobs. "JAI!"

She thrusts her mobile in my face and I scan the screen: Georgie.SUL SWHT.Luv U.Jai xxxxxx

For one moment I can't tell what it means. I've been without my mobile for so long it's like a code I can't recognize.

"Look, look!" Bianca whimpers. "'Georgie. See you later, sweetheart. Love you. JAI!' It was for Georgie Daniels, but he sent it to me! WAAAAAAH!"

And then Bianca tears herself from my arms, leaps down a flight of stairs with amazing speed and runs along the path winding beside the river. I see her pause under a streetlight long enough to fling her mobile into the inky depths of the river. Carmelita and I grab at each other's hands and are squeezing tight when we hear a far-off, depressing *plop*.

Saturday. 9:30 p.m.
PM. AW. PCC.

"BIANCA! BIANCA!" Carmelita has screeched Bianca's name so many times she's almost lost her voice.

As I stomp through the long dewy grass beside the path and poke under every bush looking for Bianca I'm thinking of Tilly's gorgeous silver sandals. They're utterly ruined and she will go absolutely mental.

"Where's that idiot gone?" asks Carmelita, for the millionth time. "We probably should go back and tell Fergie we can't find her. Why, oh why didn't I remember to pick up my phone on the way out?"

We're now so far along the river that it'll take another half-hour to walk back and our feet are already blistered. Carmelita couldn't fit her phone into her tiny evening bag, so it must be on the floor underneath a chair back at the boathouse. Brilliant! If only I had mine! This is exactly what I've been trying to tell Mum and Dad – that I need it in case of an emergency. And an emergency is what we've got right now. What if Bianca's fallen in the river? Although we would have heard a splash and a screech, surely, and we haven't heard a thing. Bianca has just vanished! Where could she have gone?

"We should try to find a pay phone and ring your parents, Els. I wouldn't be surprised if Fergie's already been on to them, we've been gone so long. This is a nightmare! BIANCA! BIANCA!"

We push our way through dark prickly bushes that tear at our frocks and stumble out onto the deserted road that runs through the park. We start looking for a phone.

"What is it with Jai anyway?" Carmelita asks, as she pads down the asphalt in bare feet, her red stilettos dangling from one hand. "Why's he always chasing the Year Twelve girls? Like that sleazoid has a chance!"

I feel really bad for Bianca. I remember how awful I felt about Will and I know she must be so upset. Could I have stopped it? I've constantly been wondering if I should have told her everything I heard about Jai. Would Carmelita have told her if the three of us were still hanging around together?

"Well, Els, it's really hard," sighs Carmelita. "It's not like you had actual evidence he was going behind her back – not before tonight anyway. Besides, Jai would have denied it and then Bianca would have totally hated your guts. In the end you just have to stay out of it, I suppose."

I have to agree. There's no logical reason for who you fall in love with. I probably shouldn't have told Bianca that Jai was no good for her. After all, she never complained about Will to me. Maybe I'll tell her I'm sorry when we find her.

"You mean *if* we find her!" Carmelita groans. "BIANCA!"

And then it starts to rain.

We walk for another twenty minutes with our evening bags on our heads to try to keep the rain off, but it's useless of course. Our gorgeous dresses are ripped and soaked through and look like dishrags. It's creepy out here, under the sickly yellow streetlights that cast reflections in the puddles.

I can't help thinking of Will back there at the dance. He'll probably think I've seen him and decided to go home.

"I wish Henry was coming down the street on his tractor to rescue me," whines Carmelita.

We finally spy a phone booth under a massive dripping tree and we huddle under its cover, a couple of shivering, drowned rats. We search in our soggy evening bags for a few coins and then find that the coin slot is totally clogged with green chewing gum!

"There's not going to be a pay phone that works in the whole of Oldcastle," moans Carmelita, and I agree through chattering teeth.

"So, we should …" Carmelita tries to think of what we can possibly do next, and then we hear the sound of sirens blaring. We see blue and red lights flashing through the trees and in the next instant we are both frozen stiff in the blinding glare of full-beam headlights.

Saturday. 11 p.m.
PM. AW. PCC.

"You could have been abducted ... or ... *anything*," says Mum, as she pours me another hot chocolate in the Palace kitchen. We'll have to get her a mobile, Rick. Then she could have called right away and ..."

Der! What have I been trying to tell her for the past two weeks?

"Exactly right," Dad nods. "Then I wouldn't have found myself down at Oldcastle Police Station with Carmelita's parents. They were frantic! I could have come and gotten you both straight away.

"What a night! First Mrs. Ferguson rings and says you're both missing. Then I'm driving like a maniac all over town!"

"Your father and I were texting each other like mad. I was terrified, waiting here for him to call, or the police to call, or Mrs. Ferguson to call. The things I was imagining! I never want to go through anything like that again as long as I live."

At least tonight there'll be no lecture on the Days Before Mobile Phones Were Invented.

"I hope there'll be some serious questions asked," Dad continues. "And I hope Jai is expelled for taking alcohol into a place where there are Year Eights! Those kids are thirteen, fourteen years old. When I was a kid ..."

I spoke too soon. Looks like I'm going to get a lecture on the Days Before Alcohol Was Invented.

"Well at least Jayden McHaargh found Bianca and took her home," says Mum. "Imagine if she'd fallen in the river?"

I did imagine. I imagined Bianca's inflatable hair buoy being run over by a ferry or nibbled by fish. She might have been swept out to sea and bobbed all the way to the Antarctic. Despite everything, I'm glad she's OK.

"Phew! Well the main thing is you're safe. Thank God!" and Mum gives me another hug.

Then, uh-oh! Here comes Tilly, rubbing sleep out of her eyes.

"What's going on?" she mumbles.

Then she sees the two mud-covered blobs lying on the kitchen floor.

"Eleanor! My new sandals! I am going to absolutely KILL you!"

And I think that maybe being abducted wouldn't have been so bad after all.

Sunday. 9 a.m.
PM. AW. PPC.

I'm standing with Carmelita and Tenzin inside the Gummy Beach Surf Club and admiring the extraordinary sand mandala the monks have made.

It's the most divine thing I have ever seen! A huge round circle – it's got to be six feet across – in a mosaic made of this intensely colored sand contained in dozens of little pots. It's taken six Gyuto Buddhist monks ten days to create the mandala, pouring the sand from tiny metal funnels onto their drawn design – beautiful trees, animals, clouds, flowers, demons and deities and a thousand ancient symbols – all beautifully and perfectly made.

I just can't find the words to describe this creation. I look over to Carmelita and Tenzin, who are also gazing at the mandala in absolute awe.

And to think that in a moment it will all be swept away!

When Gen Lama, the oldest and most venerable monk, claps his hands to start the meditation on the mandala, we three sit on the floor behind him. I wish I could empty my head and contemplate the infinite, but I'm told that takes ten thousand hours of practice!

Instead I just hold hands with Carmelita and Tenzin and feel the warmth of their bodies flowing into mine.

I close my eyes and listen to the chanted prayers of Gen Lama and the translator telling us what he's saying. There's one thing he says that stands out for me – that unless you love yourself unconditionally, you can't offer love to anyone else.

So I surrender and forgive myself. For all the dumb and stupid things I do and say. For all the mistakes I make. For just being who I am.

"I love you, Elly Pickering" is what I tell myself and my poor battered heart says: *Thank you, Eleanor. Thank you for loving me.*

I'm surprised to feel tears sliding down my cheeks and I find that hollow part of me inside and try to fill it up with thoughts of peace and happiness.

Then I'm startled by the fierce cry of two long musical instruments blown by the monks. The cymbals crash and subside, crash and subside, like the waves breaking on the shore of Gummy Beach.

Gen Lama circles the table ringing a bell and then he leans and takes a little metal object called a *dorje* – "the sacred thunderbolt" – and cuts through the sand, dividing it into eight parts.

There's a gasp from everyone in the room. It's almost painful to see the sand mandala sliced and ruined. There must be a hundred people here and no one dares move.

Then the monks take soft brushes and sweep the sand into a glass jar.

We all tumble from the Surf Club after the monks and watch them gather on the cool, pale beach sand. It's a bright spring morning. There's a chilly breeze around and the waves are small and choppy.

"This is the best, Elly. It's so exciting! Truly," says Carmelita, as she reaches her arms around my waist and hugs me hard.

Tenzin is beside me and both of us know we are taking the first steps on a journey of a thousand miles of friendship.

Now we hear the sound of bells ringing out across the ocean.

"That's the *dorje drilbu* – the tantric Tibetan bell!" exclaims Tenzin. "We should hear more cymbals, drums and *dung chen* trumpet and Gen Lama will go down to the water's edge with the mandala sand."

I love to see his black hair bobbing, his brown face so full of passion.

We watch the monks parading down the beach as they play their instruments. I have to laugh when I realize they're wearing the colors of the Gummy Beach Surf Life Saving Club – intense saffron-yellow and deep-red – but in their long robes, sandals and tall curved headdresses they're the strangest sight that's ever been seen on this stretch of sand.

The brightly colored Tibetan national flag, which Tenzin explains is forbidden to be flown in Tibet itself, is fluttering freely on a pole above the surf safety flag.

Then Gen Lama stands with his toes in the water and tips all the sand of the mandala into the ocean. A bright smear of color floats on the surface of the water for a moment and, with the tumble of just one wave, is gone forever.

Tenzin lifts his bowed head and smiles.

"And so we have it," he says. "The entire mandala was created from memory and as long as the wisdom is passed on it will be recreated."

"I'll never forget this moment," sings Carmelita. "For as long as I live, I never will."

I'm thinking the same. There is something in me that is being reborn in this ancient ritual on this fine morning. The wind and sand are peeling off my old skin and I feel like I'm brand new.

"I have to go," says Tenzin. "We have a prayer meeting now and my family is waiting for me. But I'll send a yak for you this week if you'd like to go out to the pictures, Elly."

I laugh and I can already feel that Tenzin is my friend. He came to the Palace at 8 a.m. – like he promised – and we took the long walk up over Winchester Headland and then along the sand, past Hammerhead and on to Gummy.

We didn't stop talking the whole way. It was amazing to be

with someone who really listens to what you are saying instead of fidgeting and texting and calling someone, somewhere else, about some other thing.

Tenzin doesn't have a mobile phone or a computer. He's never had them because his parents are saving all their money for a deposit on a house. But that's not to say that he wouldn't love to have all the latest technology.

"The Students for a Free Tibet slid down the Great Wall of China on ropes and unfurled a banner that read 'One World. One Dream. Free Tibet 2008' and the video was instantly posted back to New York using the Internet," he says. "Millions of people saw it on YouTube in minutes.

"The World Wide Web is one way we can overcome the censorship of the Chinese authorities. And when I get my computer I'm going to join in the campaigning to set my country free!"

I told Tenzin that there are probably also a lot of people in Tibet who would love to hear the daily agonies of Bianca Ponsford – like when she can't decide which shoes to wear to the mall.

Tenzin laughed. He laughs at all my jokes and I think this is a very good quality in a human being!

He told me he works stacking fruit down at the Britannia Markets before school and on the weekends. Soon he'll have enough money for his computer. Soon.

Now, as he looks out to sea, I see two morning suns reflected in his dark eyes. I reach for his hand and he takes mine without hesitation.

I promise to write him a letter. I'll send it to his house via Australia Post and Russell Crowe.

"Then, until I see you again – *keep your heels down while riding your horse!*" Tenzin steps back into the sand and slaps his chest with his fist.

"Is that an old Tibetan saying?" asks Carmelita.

"Maximus Decimus Meridius! From the *Gladiator* movie. *Der!* Anyway, gotta go, there's my mum."

And with that, Tenzin is off and away, leaving me laughing like a loony. I fall back into the sand and look up at the bright blue sky and feel that my heart is being healed, reassembled, fragment by fragment.

Carmelita falls down beside me and holds my hand.

"I have to go too, darling girl," she says. "We're off to the airport soon. Back home to the macadamia nuts, Viscount and Mr. Pineapple Head Henry. I don't want to leave you because I adore you so much, but I have to go."

Then we stand and brush the sand from our clothes and I step into Carmelita's open arms and we hold each other. I know we are both wishing this moment could last forever.

I'm watching her skirt and dark curls fluttering in the breeze as she runs up the beach, and with the tumble of just one wave, she's gone.

Sunday. 1 p.m.
PM. AW. PPC.

"Now, now, now, Libby! It's my money and I'll do what I like with it. And this is what I've decided to do," says Nan.

"But ... but ..." Mum protests.

"That's enough. Thank you, dear. All comments dutifully noted," says Nan firmly. Mum swallows her next comment and is quiet.

I'm standing in Nan's tiny dining room with an embroidered linen napkin tied over my eyes. I can't see a thing.

"Are you ready, Eleanor?" Nan whispers in my ear.

Well, it's hard to know what she's asking. But I trust Nan with all my heart, so ...

Yes, I'm ready!

"Ta-da!"

The napkin is whipped from my eyes, and there on top of the table are two huge boxes. I see in a heartbeat that they contain two whopping computers! *Gasp!*

"The boy at the mall told me they're the very latest. All the bells and whistles," says Nan proudly. "One for me and one for you, Elly."

I am stunned. Just ... utterly ... totally ... stunned.

"I'm told that if I get it set up I can be on the line in minutes," says Nan. "Then I just have to play these thingies here –" Nan holds up a couple of CDs – "and by this afternoon we'll both be on FacePlace and e-mail. What an excitement!"

I still can't get my mouth to form One. Single. Word.

"Of course, you'll have to share with Matilda. With all her exams coming up, she's going to need a new machine. But think of the fun we'll have, darling. I'll just go and get the camera and we'll be able to offload the pictures."

Nan scurries off to the oak dresser in the sitting room and I can hear her pulling out the drawers and rummaging madly.

"It's *upload*, Mother," calls Mum. "Not *offload*. And you'll need a digital camera."

"A what?" Nan calls back.

"A *digital* camera. Dad's old camera takes film. I'll buy you a new one for your birthday. In the meantime, come back here and let me take a couple of snaps on the mobile."

Nan comes back again and herds me into shot in front of the table. She pulls me close.

"Stand straight, Eleanor dear."

Mum snaps away.

Later, when I look at the four pictures I see:

1. I am so shocked – as if I have discovered a funnel-web spider in my slippers.

2. I am burying my face into Nan's bosom with gratitude and she's trying to peel me off her and make me face the camera.

3. I am bawling my eyes out and the light through the window catches a shiny trail of my snot.

4. I am grinning like a total idiot.

In fact, Jai could get hold of these pics and put them on FacePlace and I wouldn't care … That's how sublimely happy I am.

Later I stand with Nan in the driveway as Mum packs my new computer into the back of the car.

What about our letters, I ask my Nan. I've just discovered letters and I want us to keep corresponding by snail mail.

"Oh, we must keep writing to each other!" says Nan.

"And by the way, your handwriting tells me you are a wonderful, precious girl – thoughtful, strong, independent and loving – but then again, I didn't need to be a graphologist to know that, did I? You are everything your grandfather could ever have wished for."

Sunday. 8 p.m.
PM. AW.

My brand new computer is now set up, sitting in pride of place in The Dungeon.

Dad and Mum stand back with their arms around each other and admire it as if they have just brought a new baby sister home from Prince John Hospital.

"She's a good, big size," says Dad.

"Very smart looking, the latest operating system, lots of applications. I think we'll have her for a long time," Mum smiles.

I get online and go to FacePlace and see there are eighty-seven messages on my mirror. I'm about to read them all when it dawns on me that not one of them can really change my life in any way – the good, the bad, the ugly or the anonymous.

I have to remember what Will said: *Anything on there's not really real*, although it sure feels like it sometimes.

Then I spy a message from Nan123. How about that? (The time I spent this afternoon teaching Nan about FacePlace seems to have paid off.)

It reads: 123yhsajhsa795nb.

Too funny! Obviously it's going to take a little while for Nan to get the hang of things.

I trash everything.

I'm considering emailing Karen Crenshaw and getting her to send me the *Posh Post* documents so I can get up to speed for this latest edition (which is due to be distributed in *three days*. Yikes!) and then I have a *brilliant* idea.

I get out my pens, ink and some clean sheets of paper and I write: MY LIFE BY YAK – A JOURNEY THROUGH A POST-TECHNOLOGY LANDSCAPE.

I write four hundred words about this past two weeks, dipping into the inkwell – all the things I've heard, seen, considered, rejected, learned. Then I scan it, save it in a PDF and email it to Karen so she can knock up a layout for the *Posh Post* pages. (Hey! No point in being a complete cavewoman.)

I'm almost off to bed when Tilly barges into The Dungeon and asks if she can see my new computer. She's got just a few hours left before her first HSC exam tomorrow morning.

"It's a good unit, Els," she nods. "Hope you're not thinking of using it for the next few weeks. Consider it the first installment on my ruined shoes."

To the sound of slurping coffee, the crunch of an entire box of chocolates and low strangulated moans of frustration, I drift off to sleep.

Monday. 12:30 p.m.
PM. AW.

All of Year Twelve is off at exams today at the Exhibition Hall in Old Oldcastle and there's an air of mourning about the school – like we've waved our best and brightest off to war and we await further news from the front line.

I haven't seen Will around today, but then again, I haven't been looking for him. If he wants to see me, he can find me.

There's something that Nan told me yesterday in her tiny kitchen that I can't forget – that if Will had been desperate enough to give me the ring Lily made and tell me he loved me, even the impenetrable winter passes of the Snowy Mountains wouldn't have stopped him.

I'm back in the school library in the same sunny spot

by the window and loving reading more of *Jane Eyre*.
Our lives are so different, of course, but I do admire her
determination to have love on her own terms. It was Tilly
who first told me not to be a doormat – and I'm not going
to be.

I look up and spot Mr. York peeping through some
shelves. He peers at me over his glasses, smiles and *sallies
forth*.

"Eleanor, I was told I'd find you here. Lovely spot." He
sits in the chair opposite, fiddles with his navy school tie and
begins again with a small "Ahem."

"Firstly, I want you to know how grateful Mr. Battenburg
and I are for your efforts on Saturday night. And for
Carmelita's as well. Your evening was certainly ruined and
we are sincerely sorry. Mrs. Ferguson should never have
left you in charge of an intoxicated person. She's having
some, er, counseling about all that. I hope you'll accept our
apology."

I nod graciously. Very *Jane Eyre*. *Most Inscrutable. Deeply
Venerable*. Hah! I think I'm going to enjoy this convo.

"Secondly, I want you to know that Jai won't be
returning to Oldcastle High. His parents have elected to
move him to Britannia Boys' High, and of course his brother
Jayden will be leaving us after the exams. I can only think
that's a good thing."

Good? It's *genius!*

"Thirdly, Bianca Ponsford's with the school principal as

we speak and we shall soon be learning her fate."

Oooh! Confiscating her hair spray and teasing comb would be a good start. At least the rest of us will be spared the daily horror of her hairdressing travesties.

"Fourthly, I can't overestimate how much the whole teaching staff values you as a good influence on Bianca. There is, of course, a rogue element at this school – I'm sure most schools have the same experience – but we think Bianca's more misguided and impulsive than anything, so ... if you could ..."

Don't worry, I assure him. I'm stuck with Bianca. She's like a bungee pal and will keep bouncing back at me for the rest of my life. Don't ask me how I know. I just know.

"And *finally* ..." says Mr. York, exhaling mightily and pulling at his tie with relief. "I just had to find you and tell you how much I enjoyed your article for the *Posh Post*. It rocks, dude!"

He holds his hand to my face in what I'm guessing he thinks is a funky high-five. I slap him back.

"On this one article alone I'm happy to give you an 'A' for English this term," he says. He does look genuinely thrilled.

"Keep it up, Elly. You're a clever girl. Put your head down and get as much as you can from Oldcastle High. Don't be distracted and, like I said, I'll be reading those articles and books one day that say: *By Eleanor Pickering*. I'll be the proudest old English teacher in the world."

Do you believe that? Do you believe what just happened? Just goes to show, the crummy old library is now where the action is at Oldcastle High.

Jacaranda tree? Huh? What jacaranda tree?

Monday. 4:30 p.m.
PM. AW.

I regally descend the steps of the Royal School Bus and stroll up the purple-carpeted street to Buckingham Palace. I'm still on a high from my "A" for English and it's as if I am being escorted by Her Majesty's heralds blowing trumpets jubilant.

I greet the Duchess Camilla sitting on our fence with a generous acknowledgement and splendid pat. And the Hon. Harry the Dog – *marvelous to see you too. Good and faithful hound!*

My elegant parade comes to a sudden halt when I see Dad pull up in the driveway in an Ascot Courier van.

Dad's never home at this time of day and the thought strikes me like a thunderbolt that he's gotten the sack. When

253

I see him jump from the driver's door onto the concrete, all the elation of the day drains away and gurgles down the gutter by the curb.

Then I notice he's waving frantically with one hand and opening the back of the truck with the other.

"Elly, Elly! It's an express courier parcel from Britannia Mall," Dad shouts. "It came in to the office just now. I walked out the door so I could I deliver it personally."

I run down the sidewalk towards my smiling dad – King of all Dads, Best in the World – and before I even get to the front gate I see he's holding a large parcel. Judging by its size and shape, I think I know what's in it!

Dad and I take an end each. We rip and tear through layers of plastic, then coarse paper and down to snowy tissue. I glimpse butter-yellow, as if a newborn chick is breaking through the shell of a brown egg.

It's my handbag! My good and perfect, cute handbag!

I immediately fish inside and – OH! IT'S MY MOBILE!

Dead as a doornail, of course, but it's actually here, in its gold mesh cover, in my palm. The weight and size of it are perfect. The divine dangle of trinkets and charms that I love so much tickles the back of my hand and starts my fingers tingling.

Then, after diving back into my bag and sifting through a half-finished pack of spearmint gum, two mints stuck to a bit of tissue, an empty tube of sunscreen, two fluorescent tampons, a dried apple core, a student card and a handful of loose change comes – MY RING!

MYRINGMYRINGMYRING!

AAAAAARGH! I'M DANCING. I'M DANCING!

I notice Dad frantically pawing through the discarded pile of wrapping on the ground. He comes up with a note and hands it to me.

Dear Ms. Pickering,

I'm the Manager of Tiara Fashions at Britannia Mall and have been away on holiday for the past fortnight.

Your bag was found here two weeks ago and kept for safe storage in the stockroom by my staff. I am sorry that it was not located earlier.

As soon as I arrived at work this morning and found it, I sent it on to you by courier.

My apologies for any inconvenience.

Yours sincerely,

Sophie Rhys-Jones-Windsor

No, there's been no inconvenience, Sophie! My life's just been taken apart, stone by stone, and reassembled on the banks of Lake Eucumbene in a new and unfamiliar configuration. But apart from that, there's been no inconvenience *at all*.

"There's something else I have to tell you … And it's great news," Dad grins. "The firm's just been taken over by Commonwealth Couriers and all our jobs have been guaranteed for two *whole* years!"

Dad sweeps me into his arms and waltzes me down the street. My feet don't touch the ground until I land back in front of our crazy carriage mailbox.

"See you later, *ma belle*." He kisses me on both cheeks. "Got to get back, there's a celebration at the pub tonight. Now we can ring each other. I'll ring you … and you can ring me!"

He jumps into the front seat and roars back out the driveway. The van hiccups, shoots a cloud of black smoke and is gone from view.

This is the best news – beyond Jai leaving, Mr. York's "A" and Jane Eyre marrying Mr. Rochester. ('Cos she will. I know she will!)

What could make this day more perfect?

And. Then. I. See. It.

In the mailbox.

It's an envelope. Addressed to me. In handwriting that is tall and straight and even, and of course I know who it's from.

It's from William James Phillips and he's chosen a Cate Blanchett stamp to get this sea-blue envelope to me. He's done it on purpose because he knows that I've always wanted a missive from Galadriel, Queen of the Elves.

I sit between the two plaster lions at either side of our front steps. My hands are shaking so much I can barely get the envelope open.

My Darling Elly,
I wish I was better with words. But you know I'm not. I'm good with waves and wind and sun and sky and stuff, but words always make me feel like a grommet in two-foot slop.
I just need to say that I miss you. I miss you heaps.
Without my little leg rope, I'm a goner.
Stone cold.
I know I never told you I love you, but, hey, I'm telling you now.
I love you.
Maybe when you're next on Hammerhead and you see me paddling out, you'll blow me a kiss. Sweet!
Will. X
PS: And this ring is for you.

I shake the envelope and out falls the prettiest little thing. A small circle of gold decorated with emerald colored stones. Dark emeralds the exact color of my eyes.

Before I know it I am running up Buckingham Street to

Winchester Headland. I'm taking the old stone steps three at a time and it's like I am being swept along in the translucent barrel of a wave.

My life is spinning, spinning around me.

I wish on an emerald starfish that swishes in front of my eyes.

I put my hand to the glorious colors of the sand mandala tumbling in the foam, only to see them run though my outstretched fingers.

The waters of the Snowy River wash a flood of red roses at me, but I keep on, fighting my way through a tide of petals.

I am coming! My banners and flags flying. My drums and gongs sounding.

I am flying, swimming, running and the only thing I can hear is the *thud, thud* of my heart and my steady, buoyant breath.

And then I reach the top of the stairs. I land on the grass, all feet and arms, clumsy consonants, and exclamations. But no question marks today. Just answers. And every single one of them is "yes."

"Elly!" he calls.

I see that familiar form, not looking out to sea this day, but looking back at me.

"Will!" I echo.

And then we're together and kissing. Eye2eye. Heart2heart.

And everything's right with the world.

There's a celestial *ping* and I see we have a message from eternity@forever.com.

<u>Re: Elly and Will.</u>

Glad to see you two together again.

Blessings upon you both.

Best wishes,

The Universe *and everything*

If you no longer wish to receive these emails, please reply to this message with "Unsubscribe" in the subject line.

Saturday. 7:30 p.m.
Two weeks later.

"Smile," says Nan, as she pokes her new digital camera in my direction for what seems like the millionth time.

This evening at Eugenie's there can't be a human or one of the five elements – wood, fire, earth, water and metal – that hasn't been ambushed by Nan with her new digital camera.

All the possible human configurations have been recorded in full color:

- Libby and Rick
- Tilly and Eddie
- Carmelita and Henry

- Elly and Will
- Tenzin and Elly and Carmelita
- Libby and Rick and Elly and Tilly
- Will and Rick and Eddie and Tenzin and Henry
- Carmelita and Elly and Tilly and Mum and Pookie
- Auntie Marg, Uncle Charlie, cousins Anne and Andrew.

Can you believe my Nan's invited all my best friends to come via FacePlace? I'm half-expecting the Prime Minister to walk in the door at any moment.

And then there's crazy Bianca yakking nonstop on her mobile. My own little leg rope. The person who texted me every five minutes for the past two weeks she was in detention with Fergie.

☹ :***-) :^{} :~~) LTSGT2GTHR LUWAMH!!!

Whatever that means! I figure Bianca's here to remind me that friendship's not easy – or love, for that matter. I still wish Will talked more and I still wish I didn't ask so many questions – but we're all imperfect.

Like my new best friend Tenzin told me just this morning:

We are what we think.
All that we are arises with our thoughts.
With our thoughts we make our world.

Buddha

I grab my mobile and take some pics of Bianca. (Which means that I have copyright – heh heh!)

- Bianca with a lantern on her head.
- Bianca on her mobile with a lantern on her head and poking out her tongue.
- Bianca texting with a lantern on her head.
- Bianca showing the photo of her and Hugh Jackman (now downloaded to her phone!).
- The back of Bianca's hair, which looks like spaghetti with pesto – but it's not the quality of the photo. That's actually the color of her hair(!).

Nan hands her camera to Uncle Charlie and before we know it we all see ourselves in a slideshow on a big screen on the restaurant wall. We are reliving moments that only just happened.

When the pic of me and Will kissing comes up, we get a cheer from the crowd.

"Sweet," says Will and kisses me again.

I'm having the best time ever. There's been a bit of a mix-up in the place cards because my calligraphy still looks like roadkill. But we've worked it out and no one wants to stay in one place anyway.

I'm in charge of the music for $5 an hour (discount rate) and there's a moment in between Beyoncé and Beatles tracks (I have to cater for all tastes) when I look around and see that everyone I love the most is here – all under the same roof.

Mum and Dad are dancing and, of course, making a hideous spectacle of themselves. I've been trying to record every tragic moment with my camera for future blackmail purposes, but the light's too low, so I'm attempting to commit the crime to memory.

Watching the busy comings and goings beneath the lanterns, I'm reminded of the intricate patterns of the sand mandala. One day we will all be swept away, but the beauty of this moment will be remembered by all who saw it and the wisdom will be handed down.

I see my Nan wearing a pretty top she's sewed from her wedding dress, especially for tonight, and offering a platter of homemade curry puffs (I sent her the recipe on an eye2eye). My darling Will is loading his paper plate and kissing Nan.

I do so love my boy.

I spot the framed picture of my dear pop on a counter. Grandma and Grandpa Pickering are talking with friends, nodding and smiling, remembering him. All Nan's friends are here and they are marveling at the antique cut crystal vases spilling with masses of fragrant red roses. I have to congratulate Mum – she's outdone herself tonight.

I spy Carmelita, Tenzin and Henry giggling in the corner and Tilly looking at Eddie with bright, loving eyes.

My very own Auntie Marg from Toolewong is reading

Bianca's tarot cards at the table – and Bianca's still texting!

Then Nan insists on standing on a rickety chair to say a few words. Dad helps her up and we all gather round.

"Thank you all for being in my life," says Nan.

Brring. Brring!

Bianca's mobile rings and we all give her the evil stare.

"If my darling Andy were here today by my side," Nan continues, "he would say: Nothing lasts forever. Be in the moment. Follow your bliss, my darlings. Laugh as long as you have a breath in you. Love as long as you live."

The entire extended Royal Family of Buckingham Street raise their glasses and toast Good Queen Nan.

Hip, hip, hooray!

And long may we all live!

Acknowledgements

Sincere thanks to all the wise and wonderful women at Random House for helping me to realize this book – the redoubtable Margie Seale, the ever enthusiastic Linsay Knight and of course the very clever and insightful Kimberley Bennett.

The coven at HLA – Carolina Walkington, Jean Mostyn and Kate Richter – have also been there at every turn with words of encouragement and administrative support.

My dearest friend Hilary Linstead has been a wonderful sounding board and brought her passion to this project – as she has done, unfailingly, to all my endeavors for some twenty years now. Thank you, dearest Hil.

Thanks too to my friend Meredith Jaffe and her clever daughters for casting their expert eye over my story in the early days.

As always, my dear husband Brendan has been my very own Winchester Headland. My rock.

And to my two dear little leg ropes, Marley and Maeve – I hope this book finds its way into your box of treasures.